The Nearness Of You

The Nearness Of You

By

Mike Hutton

Blackie & Co
Publishers Ltd

A BLACKIE & CO PUBLISHERS
PAPERBACK

First published in 2003

A CIP catalogue record for this title is available from the British Library

ISBN 1 903138 82 5

Blackie & Co Publishers Ltd
107-111 Fleet Street
LONDON EC4A 2AB

To Lesley, Lucy, Kate, Chloë and Penny –

the women in my life!

CHAPTER 1

The only woman that I ever loved died in the arms of another man on September 2nd 1939. It is an easy date to remember, being the day before the outbreak of war. They were found after the fire was brought under control, scorched and locked in an obscene, macabre embrace, their bodies blackened and charred. For months I was distraught and obsessed. Lately, it is only in an unguarded moment that memories creep into my consciousness, as sharp and as painful as ever.

Now, over 60 years later, I receive a letter that is to change my life; at least, the little time that is surely left of it. After all these years, it seems bizarre that a major television company is keen to make a documentary on my life. I have lived in increasing obscurity and reduced means in Spain for the last 30 years. An unremarkable life, of increasing immobility. As age takes its toll on my activities, so it is that my small group of friends have been systematically culled by illness and death.

Maria has been with me from almost the first day I sought refuge here from the foul British weather and the pressing tax authorities. She had been a young woman then. Attractive, in a dark, rather coarse way. Good breasts, sturdy legs and a face that glowed and glowered depending on mood. We had a brief affair. It was still almost obligatory for me, even in those days. Sad, in retrospect; but, then, much of my life – when viewed dispassionately – has been. Our coupling was short-lived and unsatisfactory for both of us, and yet somehow it cleared the air sufficiently for her to adopt her current role of housekeeper, nurse, confidante and friend. When I told her of the proposed documentary, she scoffed. Mention of my past always annoys her. Even the releases, on CD, of recordings made back in the thirties and during the war are stored out of sight within days of their arrival. The only concession to my previous fame is a photographic study of me, taken at Romano's, immaculate in white tie and tails. I sit at the grand piano staring dreamily into the mid-distance, teeth flashing in a fixed smile. It is almost possible to smell the Brylcreem and cologne.

The producer of the proposed programme came to visit me within weeks of the initial approach. She was of a type I had become increasingly aware of on my annual visits to London: intelligent, single-minded, classless and seemingly sexless. Her accent had a strange cockney twang, which occasionally lapsed into an attractive, well-modulated voice. In my day it was the other way round! At first she appeared unattractive, not helped by shapeless, yet doubtless expensive, clothes. Her hair was cut savagely short and she wore a nose stud. I was reminded of wartime collaborators in France and Belgium. Even at my advanced years I am not fooled. She could be a striking-looking woman, but for reasons best known to herself she has opted for strict neutrality.

Maria took one look at Stephanie Aston and decided she hated her. She served us rancid, cold coffee and stale biscuits. I could read the signs – the theatrical sighs and the banging of the coffee mugs.

"I think we will lunch out!"

"Please yourself," she snapped, slamming the door behind her and immediately turning the radio to full volume.

* * * * * * * *

We ate at my favourite fish restaurant, overlooking the sea. It was expensive and I had rarely visited it lately. Outside the tourists peered in as they ambled by, their faces showing resentment at the sparse gathering of customers paying such exorbitant prices. The restaurant was the last outpost of what had once been an exclusive resort. Over the years it had become seedy and run-down. Now, the seafront is lined with cheap tourist hotels, noisy discos and fast food restaurants.

The money I was offered for the making of the programme was derisory, but I was to stay in first-class accommodation whilst in England and, anyway, I was flattered. I signed the contract right there in the restaurant, although Stephanie advised me to have my lawyer run through it first. She had to be kidding! His fee would be greater than mine.
I asked her when the filming would start and was told as soon as possible. I think she's worried that I might 'snuff it'.
She arranged for a camera crew to come out in a fortnight's time, and then it would be straight over to London. It was only when she had left for the airport and Maria had gone to her bedroom in a sulk that doubts began to form in my mind. There were many good times to be recalled, but also memories that had taken great resolve and possibly downright cowardice to hide away.
The filming in Spain took only a day and I was amused to note that Maria had been to the hairdressers and was wearing her favourite dress, one that I had bought for her at Liberty's. Her initial antagonism to the project had vanished and she engineered an appearance in almost all the clips.
Acquaintances often declare that I am remarkable for my age, but that is when they see me in the warmth of the Spanish sun. London in October is wet and misty. Within hours of my arrival the damp invades my joints. My hands swell up, with knuckles so large that it is difficult for me to hold my ebony cane. By the time we reach the Hampshire Hotel in Leicester Square my feet are refusing to react to the signals from my brain. I struggle to get out of the car, but they stubbornly remain stuck under the front seat. The doorman has to wrestle them free, and I stagger unsteadily to reception. I am disappointed not to have been put up at the Ritz or Savoy, where I have performed and am known. The building now occupied by the Hampshire had been either apartments or office accommodation in my heyday. At least they have

booked me a suite: a small, relatively modest one, but comfortable enough, and satisfyingly warm.
I am given the remainder of the day to rest before filming starts. The plan is to take me to some of my old venues and film me with a couple of ageing contemporaries, although I can scarcely remember them. The London filming is to take two days, but then comes the bombshell. It is proposed that we should then all travel to Great Theddington, the village where I grew up and lived until I went to London. This I really don't want to do, but I am referred to the small print in the contract. The thought of returning to Theddington fills me with dread. I even contemplate feigning illness; and yet here, at last, is a chance to make peace with a part of my life that has gnawed away at my subconscious; an opportunity to record objectively the real story, most of which – I imagine – will not even be touched upon by programme-makers.

* * * * * * * *

I don't leave the hotel. I sleep all afternoon and then have supper in my room. I watch some inane television into the early hours. Annoyingly, now that most people are asleep, I feel wide awake. The thought of having a bath appeals, but the sides of the impressive tub look far too high for me to negotiate without Maria's help. Slowly I shed my clothes. My suite is a mass of mirrors. I can't avoid seeing my body: a parody of its former self. Acres of white translucent skin, the texture of communion bread, dried and spent. Varicose veins run down my stick-like legs, whilst my buttocks, once so round and firm, are reduced to wrapping paper – only just containing bones that press urgently for attention. My small, soft belly protrudes in front of me, the last acknowledgement of the good life I have lived. When young we preen and pose in front of the mirrors, but in old age the reflections magnify our increasing frailty and ugliness. I manage to negotiate the power shower, its jets hitting me like tracer bullets. Then, dressed in hotel bathrobe, I lie back on the bed, but still sleep eludes me. I shuffle over to the minibar. I have almost given up alcohol over the past couple of years. Even the finest wines have started to taste sour and vinegary. I pour a mini-bottle of Glenmorangie into a cut crystal glass and, taking a sip, I shudder. My apprehension is lifting. I am opening my heart and my mind. I can sense her. She is still a long way off but she is there, I know. At the moment I am not sure if my tears are of sadness or joy. Am I fearful or about to become liberated?

CHAPTER 2

How many faces do we see in the course of a lifetime? Hundreds of thousands, possibly even millions. Who knows? Each one different, an infinite variation on a theme. Some faces we remember as they were when we first met, particularly when we are in nostalgic mood. We can unravel the years, deny the changes that ageing brings. A few faces improve with age, but most that have once been a source of admiration or envy either pinch or coarsen.

The face I now find easiest to conjure up I never saw. At least, not in the flesh. Yet, looking back, am I even certain of that? A memorable face, though. One of haunting beauty, captured in a painting I found whilst helping to decorate my mother's bedroom in anticipation of my father's return from the trenches. He had been back from France for some three months, at first in a hospital in Southampton, before being moved along the coast to Worthing. Connie, my mother had been down to see him once, but the train connections were difficult and the fare expensive. Several men from the village had been killed in the war and others severely injured. It was a period of worry and grief for everyone, countered by a communal stoicism. My mother had been evasive about his injuries on her return and unusually withdrawn; for the first time in my young life her thoughts seemed to exclude me.

Some weeks later a letter arrived informing her of my father's actual homecoming. This threw her into a frenzied bout of spring-cleaning. Flımsy curtains were washed, sheets changed, and linoleumed floors scrubbed. My dad had been a farm labourer before the war. We had all lived in one of a row of tiny tied cottages. Within weeks of my father's departure we were given notice by his employer, a thin, dark-skinned farmer with huge mutton chop whiskers. He needed the accommodation for my father's replacement, and he informed anyone who cared to listen that he was also fighting a war, just to keep his head_above water. It was true; he worked all the hours God gave and was not much better off than we were. It appeared we would have to go and live with relatives in Derbyshire, until the rector approached my mother to take over as his housekeeper following Mrs Howarth's recent untimely death.

It was partly my growing up in the rectory that led to my scepticism and distrust of religion, particularly Christianity. A long life has not led me to believe differently. The Reverend Beresford Egan was a short, stout man with a florid complexion and a shiny bald head. His fleshy face was made to beam, his belly to heave with laughter. At first glance he looked like a merry monk, the type you find today on humorous Christmas cards. He was, though, a man who exuded gloom. Mirth was unknown to him, a smile was rarely seen on his face, and then translated more into a look of pain. He was not a bad man and in truth he reflected the atmosphere of the village in those far-off days.

The rectory stood next to the ancient church of St Helen's. It was largely of red brick construction, built in the high Gothic tradition. We lived in a tiny, older part of the house made up of mellow Northamptonshire stone. Our quarters could be approached only by the back door. The accommodation was also separate, with just one connecting door to the main house. It was stark by comparison; our only concession to modern living was running water – unlike most of our neighbours, who had to rely on drawing it from deep sinister wells.

It was at that time that I remember watching my mother trying on dresses that I had never seen before. She posed, pirouetting in front of the cracked mirror in her bedroom. She had persuaded the vicar to let her have some whitewash and a dark green paint stored in the coach house, as the bedroom was not suitable for a man deprived of a proper home for the past three years. It faced north – dark and damp, and in my childish mind strangely forbidding. The window frames were

rotten, soft to the touch and covered in peeling brown paint. The wallpaper had probably been attractive once. Now the small bunches of flowers that formed the pattern were dulled, stained and speckled with mildew. Behind the brass bed the paper was torn and ragged. It was a sad room. I watched my mother as I half-heartedly rubbed down the skirting boards with a rough sandpaper. My earliest memories of her were of a bonny, handsome woman with a comforting bosom for a young boy to cuddle up to. She was calm, giving me a feeling of security. She had a smell all of her own. A well-scrubbed smell, of Pears soap and a hint of recent cooking. Most of the smells of my childhood have gone – floated off in time.
My father's absence and the worries of war had somehow diminished Connie. Not in spirit or resolve, but, physically, weight had fallen from her. She seemed small, even to a seven-year-old. Her movements had changed. Fast and jerky, everything done in a hurry. I didn't understand then about the huge demand the vicar put on her. She worked for pitiful wages, but he expected a full 14-hour day in return. Perhaps this is why, for much of the time, she appeared preoccupied and stressed; but when she did relax she was beautiful. She would sit on my bed each evening, reading me a story whilst slowly brushing her long brown hair. She brushed it exactly 100 times, a slow continual movement, her voice and the brush in harmony. She always wore her hair up in a bun when she was working, making her look much older, but even so I noticed the tradesmen flirted with her. Even Reverend Egan was marginally less austere in her presence, but I gathered he was being awkward about my father coming home. He had taken my mother in "out of the goodness of his heart," I heard him tell her, and this had not been intended to extend to my father. In retrospect, I think he assumed my father would be killed. The matter was left unresolved. The concession of the decorating materials at least indicated that we were unlikely to be thrown onto the streets in the short term. He became

increasingly demanding and grumpy, though, and I tried to avoid coming into contact with him. He worked my mother even harder, seeming to resent the decorating of the bedroom.
I was making slow headway with the rubbing down, so I was handed a knife to help strip the wallpaper. Progress was still slow, even with the help of warm soapy water. Some of the paper parted from the wall in long strips as if liberated, but mostly it had to be coaxed away in small, shredded pieces.
"What have we here, boy?" My mother had been stripping great swathes of paper from behind the tiny fire grate. In the corner of the room she had exposed a small wooden door. She ran her knife round the perimeter, cutting away the encrusted paint. She flicked a small wooden catch on the door and tried to prise it open, going quite red in the process. A larger, more solid knife was brought from the kitchen. It seemed likely the blade would snap when suddenly the door shot open, particles of dust and paint momentarily clouding our vision. The opening was too small for my mother to get anything but her head and shoulders through, so I was dispatched to explore. The air was dry and oppressive as I edged further into the gloom, the floorboards hard against my bare knees.
My mother went downstairs to get a candle. As I waited for her return I heard a noise somewhere ahead of me. Probably just a bird, or a mouse. Then it occurred to me it might be a rat. I was terrified of rats, I had nightmares about them. I started back in fright, my leg catching something soft. I groped about, still staring forward, convinced that some giant rat was waiting for its moment to attack me. I gathered up a bundle of papers and reversed out into the bedroom as quickly as I could. I handed my mother the small bundle of what appeared to be letters – a dozen or so, tied with a blue ribbon. The envelopes were splattered with bird droppings and the writing on the envelopes had faded with age. Leaving Connie to examine them, I was propelled back into the cupboard, the

candle casting eerie shadows. My imagination conjured up images of monsters and dead bodies. “Is there anything else in there?” my mother demanded.
“No, it’s empty.” I just wanted to get out.
“Take a good look, mind.”
“There’s nothing; I’m coming out.” There was a fresh rustling from the far darkness, a flapping of what sounded like giant wings. I swear I heard a cry. I turned, lurching, seeking the comfort of the dim light coming from the bedroom. The candle flame was flickering from a draught that had not been noticeable previously. I tried to adjust my eyes to the changing light. Eerie shadows mocked me, then to my right I spotted something solid. Edging further forward I could see what appeared to be a picture frame, propped against a cruck beam that curved and arched into darkness.
“There is something, mum.” The draught had strengthened to a breeze. The vague outlines of the ornate picture frame appeared and faded as the candle flame flickered like a dying heartbeat. Total darkness was followed by a sudden eruption. The bats flew straight at me, brushing against my face. I screamed! Not once, but a continual shriek! I was terrified, but the noise sent the bats seeking the furthest confines of the eaves.
I don’t remember dragging the picture out, but I know my mother was laughing and called me ‘a sissy’. I fled the bedroom, seeking the warmth and light of the kitchen, leaving Connie to stagger downstairs, clinging to the unwieldy picture. The scrolled frame had become begrimed during its stay in the dark recess, encrusted with years of bird droppings. The painting was protected by glass, though, and my mother wiped away at it with a dampened dishcloth. The smeared image distorted the face. It conveyed pain for those few seconds before the cloth resumed its work. The suffering of a tormented mind. A madwoman! Then, as the grime was cleaned away, another quite different image appeared.

"Oh, Bob, isn't she lovely?"
To me her face still looked sad. True, there was just the hint of a smile on her lips. It wasn't a smile conveying happiness, though; rather, the type that is prompted by someone outside the picture. The artist, perhaps? The equivalent of a photographer asking her to say 'cheese'? Maybe, though, it was an onlooker watching the artist coaxing the character to life. These were thoughts that came to me later in life, when I knew more. As a child I was less enquiring, yet sensitive enough to be aware of an overwhelming impression of vulnerability.
"Who is she, mum?"
The portrait was painted on heavy, beige-coloured paper. She had been captured from the waist up. Her robes had been conveyed in a number of bold strokes of black and white gouache. In contrast the face and veil had been carried out in the minutest detail. Black hair, each wisp recorded. High cheekbones, a fine straight nose and lips a shade too thin. The eyes, deep brown and sad, looked straight at me and through me. I moved, but they followed me. They are with me still. She had a dark spot in the centre of her forehead. I was reminded of some illustrations in my schoolbooks.
"Is she a native?" I enquired. In those non-politically correct times that was how we referred to anyone with a dark skin. In fact, all foreigners were either villains or savages – or worse. Even our allies were viewed with great suspicion.
"She's Indian, boy. A princess, I shouldn't wonder."

* * * * * * * *

I awake drained and confused. For a moment I can't remember where I am. My whisky lies untouched on my bedside table. I fuss around, looking for my pills. Seemingly with each year that passes a new pill is prescribed. Arthritis, blood pressure, anaemia, thyroid; the prescriptions lengthen and I feel worse. I know Maria packed them. She is zealous in pursuit of my longevity. I haven't left the room since I arrived. I get quite flustered, turning out drawers and checking my suitcase. Well, I shall probably feel better without them. I often threaten to stop taking them at home, but only to annoy Maria.

I have lived too long, outstayed my welcome. Memories of my childhood underline the fact. Horse-drawn carts to the Internet don't sit easily together. The two extremes of my life are incompatible. I must have been at ease somewhere in the middle, during the years of success and fame. Looking back, though, I seemed incapable of anything but the most shallow thoughts during that period. A time of 'bright young things'; sports cars, expensive clothes and the dedicated pursuit of enjoyment. Endless performances in luxurious settings. Recognition, adulation and numerous affairs. I was to be seen at Newmarket, Henley, Wimbledon. I attended championship fights at Haringey and went riding in Hyde Park. I rubbed shoulders with the rich and famous, the 'fast set' and their hangers-on. I lived on a diet of false bonhomie and vulnerable girls. Then, fleetingly, love. Gut-wrenching, helpless, love. If there is a God out there (which I still doubt), he hates us to get above ourselves. Happiness in life has to be rationed. Each coupon recorded.

My room is uncannily quiet for central London – the advantage of having a hotel in a largely pedestrianised area. I draw the curtains and look down on crowds of people arriving for another day's work, many with mobile phones clamped to their heads. A road sweeper is driving a mechanical contraption, eating up some of the rubbish left from the previous evening. Was London always so untidy? Perhaps I have a selective memory, like remembering only sunny summer days as a child. Certainly, people are less well turned out. It is no longer possible to tell a person's background by their dress. Today, it is a free-for-all. An earring and a

shaved head are just as likely to belong to a lawyer or business executive as a barrow boy.
It is strange looking out over such a familiar landscape and yet one that now seems quite foreign. I have appeared in dozens of venues within a quarter-mile radius of my hotel. The Café de Paris had been just across the square. Down in that fashionable basement I had entertained with seemingly effortless renditions of the latest songs from Noel Coward, Cole Porter and Irving Berlin. Immaculate in white tie, starched shirt, waistcoat and tails made for me in Jermyn Street and Savile Row. My handmade shoes were from Tuczon in Clifford Street and there was always a fresh buttonhole delivered each day from the florist in Burlington Arcade. My trademark white grand piano was moved from venue to venue and always topped with a single silver candelabra (copied later by that ghastly Liberace). I would usually start my act with *The very thought of you*, and by the time I reached *These foolish things* I could guarantee that a scattering of girls would be draped adoringly over the piano.
The sharp intrusive jangle of the telephone interrupts my thoughts. I am to be picked up in half an hour for the first day's shooting. My apprehension returns. I am missing Maria. She has become a major part of my life. She looks after me. I wish she had come with me. I feel lonely and vulnerable in the capital where once I was a household name.
I see the road sweeper has turned his engine off and is in earnest conversation on his mobile. What the hell does everybody find to talk about?
A group of vagrants are drinking Export lagers from cans and abusing passers-by. Raw-boned, florid and filthy, they vent their anger and frustration, but no one gives them a second glance. Just feet away a young couple are locked in a passionate embrace. Some things never change!

CHAPTER 3

I am caught unawares. The camera is rolling as the lift doors open. Like most performers, I preen and react once a camera is pointed my way. I cross the lobby, conscious of hotel guests trying to guess who this old codger could be. I stand taller, my familiar stoop banished for a moment. I twirl my cane instead of leaning on it for support. It is as if I have had an injection of adrenalin, or something stronger. My suit may be old-fashioned, but it's well cut and since my recent loss of weight it fits well. Only my shirt collar ruins the overall effect. It gapes, as if my yellow silk tie has not been tightened enough. I look like a humanised giraffe!

It is only a short car ride to the headquarters of UTV. The building is a temple to a new century: acres of tinted glass, aluminium and ugly wall panels. Grey carpets stretch down endless corridors. They have arranged a meeting room just off reception, presumably in deference to my immobility. I am seated at a long glass-topped table. The room is dominated by pale wood panelling. It reminds me of a crematorium. Careful, I am becoming obsessed with death.

I am surrounded by an earnest young team. Their number astounds me, for they are all connected with the programme. Producers, editors, researchers, technicians and make-up artists. On the surface they are informal, but so serious. Everyone makes notes and the talk is of reporting procedures. Something I have eaten hasn't agreed with me. I smile at a young man sitting opposite. It is a windy smile; my stomach cramps and churns. I feel the need to fart to release some of the gases that have built up. I draw in a deep breath and clench my buttocks. I have no wish to humiliate myself in front of this rather frightening group of youngsters. The discomfort gradually subsides. The talk is interminable, the writing extending to several pages of foolscap. They are all polite to me but I feel as if I have no control over proceedings.

I am an object, a product to be painfully shoehorned in and out of expensive cars. To be stood in front of a number of pre-selected venues, to talk with a selection of people that they have chosen. I have not been consulted on any of this. Some of the venues I hardly ever appeared at and the people played no more than a fleeting part in my life. No matter; I shall do as I am told. The day is something of a blur, but when the camera is pointed I perform. I recall those far-off days. At first I embellish the truth, sometimes lapsing into downright lies. I am amusing and scurrilous. That's show business! And, besides, there are not many people still around to query my version of events.

Crowds gather and gawp as I am filmed outside what was the Monseigneur Nightclub in Piccadilly. It is now a cinema showing X-certificate films. I recall some far worse goings-on there between a titled lady and two black musicians. Many aristocrats 'stepped over the traces' in those days. It was left to the middle classes to uphold moral values. Stephanie Aston tells me I am a natural in front of the camera. A young woman asks for my autograph. She tells me she has all my records at home. I am amazed that anyone so young should enjoy my work. I am encouraged, flattered. I am filmed kissing her. More people request autographs, but I think it is just the herd instinct. I'm not sure that half of them even know who I am.

Our next stop is outside what used to be one of London's most exclusive night spots. The Blue Train, in Stratton Street, was an exact replica of the Côte d'Azur luxury express. The entrance was illuminated by a station sign. It was a place where blue bloods from country piles rubbed shoulders with film stars. It drew in minor European royalty and American bankers, and prizefighters were welcomed, adding that dimension of danger. Even gangsters and pimps gained entry, adding to the heady brew. Noel Coward could always get a table at a moment's notice, and it was where Cole Porter used to come and see me perform when he was in town. I played in a thick haze of smoke, allowing myself two Martini cocktails during my 40-minute stints. Although I usually played without any band backing me, I did appear with Ray Noble on a couple of occasions. I became a regular drinking partner of Al Bowlly. The food, as I remember it, was good though plain by today's standards. 'Forget the cuisine, go to be seen' was the catchphrase at the time.

I am offered lunch at what used to be the Piccadilly Hotel. "Marco Pierre White," Stephanie Aston whispers to me. I look blank. Later I am told he is a famous chef. Celebrity chefs didn't exist in my day; they just cooked! Anyway, I elect to go back to my room for a rest. This afternoon it's off to the Palladium. I only ever appeared there once. What the hell!

* * * * * * * *

I never did understand why my mother handed over the painting and letters to Reverend Egan. He decreed that the writing was obscene and licentious. Accordingly the letters were consigned to the coal fire in his study, and in doing so a link was formed that became apparent to me only years later. Over half a century was to pass before I was to see the haunting image of that painting again.

Our discoveries were soon forgotten when news came through that my father had suffered a relapse. It was to be a couple of months before we were reunited. The frenzied cleaning was reduced to sensible levels. After my mother's initial disappointment, she seemed more relaxed. The vicar positively exuded well-being, even giving me the odd copper as pocket money.

Like all youngsters I lived only for the moment. My father was consigned to the back of my mind. The summer holidays were spent fishing, fruit picking and playing cricket.

Sometimes I would help some of the older boys 'bullock whacking'. Sticks in hand, we drove the cattle the four miles or so down to Stratton Market on a Monday evening. There they were left grazing in a field close to the market, so that they would look their best and fetch good prices the following morning at auction.

I could never understand why holidays rushed by and yet in term time it was as if the clocks had been tampered with, to extend the misery that was school.

So, on the first day of the autumn term, I loitered, looking for any distraction that might delay my progress. Carrying two rounds of dripping sandwiches and an apple suspended on a stick over my shoulder, I made my way slowly down the hill from the vicarage. Why is it that I can remember Theddington in those days with such clarity and yet events from my recent past elude me? The village was a dreary place then, cast down by poverty. Of course, it looked picturesque when bathed in summer sunlight. There was almost no traffic so it was very peaceful, but it certainly was not idyllic. There were rows of broken cottages and ramshackle shops. Thatched roofs were balding or green with mildew. The more pragmatic owners had covered their roofs with corrugated iron sheeting, which soon turned rusty. Lying in bed on a rainy night I would listen to syncopated rhythms, which became demented when the rain turned to hail. The war had brought hard times to much of the rural community. The overall impression was of peeling paintwork in depressing shades of browns and greens, and a road surface rutted and liable to flood even after a short shower.

As I dawdled towards the small village school, a few of the shops were opening up. There was a smell of freshly baked bread and Mr Lord the butcher was hanging huge carcasses from hooks in his small, dark premises. Behind the shop was the abattoir. A series of tin sheds, from where periodically stifled cries and ominous thumpings could be heard.

The school was a single-storey building of unfading red brick. It had a small playground at the rear overlooking the rolling countryside down to Stratton Market. There were some 30 pupils, all taught by the one teacher. Their ages ranged from five to 14. Some of the older children were appointed monitors, and were occasionally allowed to teach the youngsters.

I could hear the hubbub from the playground long before the school came into view. The noise was different, unfamiliar. I paused, listening. A sort of singing. Chanting, more like. I opened the playground gate; most of the boys were playing football, oblivious to the commotion. A few stood embarrassed, just watching. Most of the girls had formed a circle and were shouting out the words of the nursery rhyme *Ten little nigger boys*, except that under Ann Jope's direction the words had been changed to 'ten little nigger girls standing in a row!' I could just make out a small figure caught in the middle of the circle. She stood quite still, and although tiny in stature she was hunched, as if by making herself smaller still she could avoid the lyrics being directed at her. This seemed to annoy Ann Jope, who broke away from the others and started pushing the young girl and grabbing her by the hands and propelling her round. Where was Miss Ormerod? Our teacher was a martinet, who had the capacity to spread fear through even the eldest pupils. I saw her standing motionless at her study window. She stared down, her face an impassive mask.

I felt a sudden rush of rage. All of us were bullied when we started at the school. Mostly it was fairly good-humoured, but in my childish mind I knew instinctively that this was different. Sinister, frightening. Although most of the girls forming the ring were older than me, I barged through their ranks, shouting: "Leave her alone, you bullies!"

"Look what the cat's brought in," Ann Jope sneered. She was the most senior girl in school. A podgy 14-year-old, with frizzy auburn hair, a volcanic temper and a biting tongue. Even the older boys tried to keep on her right side. She was also Miss Ormerod's favourite. She towered above me, poking at my chest with a stubby finger; "Savage-lover, are you?"

"How would you like it?" I said, rather tamely. I noticed the little girl had slipped through the cordon and off to the side of the playground.

"Being called nasty names." To my alarm, tears were welling up in my eyes. Tears of frustration.

"Cry-baby bunting," she taunted. Turning to her friends she led them into a chorus, their original target for abuse forgotten. Ann Jope caught me by the ear, twisting my head round level with her chest. She smelt of stale sweat and mothballs.

"Droopy tits." I said it quietly. Not the wittiest or most cutting remark, but what do you expect from a seven-year-old? It was their close proximity and it was the first nasty thing I could think of. There was a sharp intake of breath.

"What did you say?" Her face was flushed with anger, but she really should not have asked, as I am certain she was the only one to hear my initial outburst.

"Droopy tits," I shouted at the top of my voice. Her eyes, normally two narrow slits, camouflaged by unruly hair and huge cheeks, took on new life. They bulged, opening so wide as to totally change her appearance. She let out a low howl like that of a trapped animal. She threw me to the ground, my head hitting the gravel. As she tried to grapple me to my feet again Fred Davison shouted, "Mind you don't topple over, Ann."

"Wobble, wobble," another boy giggled, and suddenly everyone was shouting 'droopy, droopy' at the tops of their voices. Ann looked confused; even her friends were joining in.

"Stop!" This was the voice we all knew and feared. "How dare you?" Miss Ormerod was shaking with rage. We were informed that we were all to be kept in after school and I was to get the strap. As we made our way to the school building I noticed Ann Jope had pulled a cardigan over her dress, in an attempt to hide the cause of her mortification. The new girl walked ahead of me into the classroom, without even giving me a second glance.

* * * * * * * *

Instinct makes it difficult to keep your hand extended as the strap descends. It's second nature to pull it away at the last moment, but I knew this would lead only to an increase in my punishment. So I closed my eyes and bit my tongue. I was not a favourite of Miss Ormerod at the time. My skill at the piano was still to make itself apparent. For excellence was what our teacher thrived on. It brought her reflected glory when the school inspectors visited. So it was that all our work had to be prepared on slates before being painstakingly transferred to exercise books. Neatness in appearance and copperplate handwriting were required from every pupil. The ability to recite poetry or to sing were also well regarded by Miss Ormerod, as was mental arithmetic. The inspectors rarely failed to be impressed by the standards produced at our small school. Miss Ormerod would colour and glow as they congratulated her. A letter of commendation from the chairman of governors would reduce her to tears.

Although she always tried to coax the best from her pupils, she found it hard to overcome her deep-rooted sense of snobbery. To her, status in life was everything; hence shopkeepers and farmers' children were looked on more kindly than their employees' offspring. Doctors and lawyers were looked up to, whilst meeting anyone loosely termed 'gentry' reduced her to an obsequious wreck. Her feelings culminated in the royal family. She was a true patriot, performing what she thought was the key task in turning out worthwhile citizens, often from very unpromising raw material. She was an amazing teacher, but a ghastly person.

Each day at school followed an identical format. It began with prayers thanking God for all the joy that he was bestowing on us. Then came a hymn selected by Miss Ormerod. On Empire Day and the King's birthday we sang the national anthem standing to attention, our teacher's face flushed with emotion. Within a year Miss Ormerod had learnt of my talent as a pianist and I then accompanied the school each morning. I was elevated in her eyes, another talent to be paraded in front of the inspectors.

After the daily hymn the register was taken with pedantic care. In a school as small as ours it was possible to spot absentees at a glance, but each name had to be carefully recorded in a large green ledger. "Kitty Curtis," Miss Ormerod called, her pen hovering over the lined page. All eyes focused on the new girl sitting at the front of the class.

"Here, madam." The assembly were reduced to a collective fit of giggles.

"'Miss', Kitty Curtis. I am not a madam." Fred Davison was heard to say: "Not much," and was sent to stand in the corridor for his pains.

The teacher then put Kitty through a cross-examination. "Where do you come from?"

"Railway House, miss."

"No, child. Where were you born?"

"Poona." More giggles from the class, silenced by Miss Ormerod's fierce gaze.

"Where is Poona, Joe?" Joe Tremlett was in his final year at school; I could never make out if he was stupid or always having fun at other people's expense.

"Just outside Rugby," he replied, straight-faced.

"You stupid boy." She hurled a piece of chalk at him, which he caught expertly above his right ear and returned it to the teacher's desk.
"Where is Poona, school?" Only Ann Jope dared reply, and she was treated to a baleful stare for her guess of 'Africa'.
"India, you dolts. Look here." She pointed to the world map pinned up next to the blackboard.
"Actually, miss, you are pointing at Delhi; Poona is just south of Bombay." Miss Ormerod looked flustered for a moment. Looking back I think our teacher doubted that her new pupil could even read. She then put Kitty through her paces the rest of us had seemingly forgotten. It was soon obvious that the little girl didn't only read, but knew poems by Wordsworth and Scott off by heart. She could recite her tables and had no trouble with her division and subtraction. Now, here was a child with great potential. Within half an hour Kitty had been transformed from a problem to a potential asset. Ann Jope and one or two others would really hate her now.
That evening there was a bang on our door. I was practising the piano; something I was allowed to do only when the vicar was out. My mother showed a small dark-haired man into our parlour. He wore a shiny suit and a stiff collar. This alone set him apart. Most men in the village wore a suit (if they had one) only to attend funerals.
"I've come to say thank you to your son. At least, Kitty has. Children can be so cruel. He was very brave."
The little girl stared at the floor. "What do you say?" her father prompted.
Looking up from the piano stool I could see she had been crying.
"Thank you," she mumbled.
She had probably been forced to come. I thought girls were pathetic. She had long eyelashes, but I couldn't tell if her tears were of sadness or anger. I had never seen eyes so dark.

They bordered on black. They drew me in. They always would. It took a conscious effort for me to look away.

CHAPTER 4

The overwhelming impression is of colour and heat. Vibrant reds, flamboyant yellows. Crowds hem me in as we jostle down a dusty street. There is no noise. The silence is eerie. The architecture is strange to me; turrets and minarets towering above humble dwellings. The light is blinding, reflected off the white walls. I am being swept along by a tide of humanity. I feel no fear. I can't fall, I am hemmed in by the crowds. The mass is heading for what appears to be a huge, slow-moving, muddy-coloured river. We descend the steep hill, running now, the sweat pouring down my chest. The crowd parts to make way for me. Someone is pushing me from behind. I want to stop but the incline is too steep. The sea of faces becomes a blur. As I reach the river a figure dressed in black raises his arms to greet me. Around his neck he wears a huge pewter crucifix. I reach out to him, but he moves aside. The river is dry. There is a yawning chasm. I am falling...

* * * * * * * * *

I can hear my heartbeat through my sweat-stained shirt. I stare up at the recessed lights in the ceiling, listening to the vague street noises from outside. My tongue feels furred and I have a disgusting taste in my mouth.

Soon after I arrived in Spain I had what was referred to at the time as 'a near-death experience', caused (I learnt later) by the carotid artery in my neck. I had been complaining of feeling ill all afternoon, but Maria had not been very sympathetic. I remember suddenly feeling very sick. I stumbled towards the bathroom but fell back onto the settee. I was feeling disorientated. I appeared to be on a moving staircase. Below me was a sort of stage with a background of the most vivid blue and in the foreground was a figure dressed in white robes. It was unclear whether this apparition was male or female. My brain was still active and I remember thinking: "What am I doing here?" Gradually I became aware of someone touching my chest and a voice, Maria's voice, almost a whisper. The hitting on my chest became harder and the voice louder. I resented the intrusion; I wanted to go to the figure in white. Then Maria's shouting broke into my consciousness; "Don't you dare leave me," she screamed. Ten minutes later I was in an ambulance.

From that time I have endured frightening images, which appear in my mind's eye without warning, usually when I am either tired or distressed. I look at the bedside clock. I haven't eaten anything. I go to the minibar and take out a bag of nuts. My shirt is quite damp, clinging to my body. I smell under my arms. I reek of age – an unhealthy odour. I can't go out like this; I will have to change. I turn on the shower. It spits at me with snake-like venom. Standing under its jets, I imagine the water washing away the years.

* * * * * * * *

Whilst my recall of events that took place over 80 years ago is vivid, their sequence is muddled. The arrival of Kitty and her parents heralded a number of important changes in my life, but in what order I honestly can't remember. These strangers continued to be the main topic of conversation in the village for months after their arrival, even allowing for the monumental historic events that were to impact on all our lives. Mr Curtis left his house each morning at seven o'clock, in a pony and trap, for Stratton Market. He had spent 15 years working on the Indian railways. As general manager of the local railway company he controlled and was responsible for stationmasters, porters, signalmen, clerks and gangers covering an area of about 20 square miles. As such, he held an important position in our small community. No one, though, seemed to know how to react to his wife. A small, solemn figure, whose bright clothes jarred and somehow irritated the locals. They knew of nothing but their own restricted lives. Nonconformity was viewed with suspicion. Foreigners posed danger. The village had trouble enough dealing with its own differences. Church of England folk shopped at premises run by members of their own denomination, whilst they were boycotted by the Baptists. Chapel and Church formed a great divide. Most friendships were made along religious lines and each side was fiercely supportive of their own and quick to criticise the wrongdoings of the opposition. An Irish Roman Catholic family, whose father worked at the hall, were dubbed papists or Fenians and barely tolerated. Strangely, a Jewish traveller who visited the village every couple of months, selling lengths of cloth, ribbons and buttons, had what my mother called 'the gift of the gab' and was able to charm ladies of all ages.

So, where was this to leave the native woman, in the eyes of the village?

Mr Curtis was well up the social pecking order, employing half a dozen men from the village alone. It was a dilemma overcome by most of the women ignoring Kitty's mother, except when accompanied by her husband. Then they were icily polite. He must have been aware of what was going on, but he never made a comment about her lack of acceptance that I can remember. My mother was about the only one to make any effort to befriend her. She felt sorry for the woman, thousands of miles away from her home. Even for Connie, though, it appeared something of an uphill battle, as she struggled to understand the strange accent of her new neighbour. Increasingly Mrs Curtis spent more time cocooned inside her house, sheltering from a climate that even in the height of summer felt cold to her. To me, as a young boy, it was if an exotic flower had been planted in our cold, damp clay.

My father finally arrived home on the first Saturday in November. I remember it being a Saturday as I was not at school, or having to attend a church service. I sat on the church wall next to our house, as it gave a good vantage point to spot oncomers as they rounded the corner. The ancient stone cut into my legs and the vicar's cross-bred terrier seemed to sense something special about the day, staring down the length of the street, his tail wagging in anticipation.

My memories of my father were dim. He had been away for over three years. I had an impression of strong arms cradling me on his lap. Of course, trousers tickling my legs and the vague smell of tobacco. Whilst excited, I was apprehensive about his return. My mother and I had settled into a routine that suited us well and I was worried I would be relegated in her affections.

'Mad' Mrs Morris, who ran the wool shop opposite our house, came out and accused me of spying on her. I thought she was an old witch, and although bent and walking with the aid of a stick she was only in her fifties. Her stock, much of it dating back to before the war, was heaped in collapsing piles, so random that it was impossible to see the counter on entering the shop. Deranged for years, she bent the few coins that were spent at the shop with rusty pliers, convinced that everyone was trying to pass counterfeit money.

Heavy clouds hung overhead and there was an unusual stillness in the air. Patch, the terrier, pricked his ears and whined. The first splatter of rain caught me unawares and I sought the protection of the trees in the graveyard. The little dog was standing in the middle of the road, his head cocked to one side. I listened too, not moving. I sensed rather than heard someone – something – coming. The hair on the little dog's back was standing on end. He gave a yelp of fright and scampered off to the safety of the rectory vegetable garden. I could hear soft footsteps on the road, like cattle being driven, but it wasn't milking time. Round the corner came a huge, dark creature. I wanted to run, but I stood transfixed. It moved with the grace of a ballroom dancer, its massive ears wobbling with each step. Behind, a baby hung onto its mother's tail. A huge trunk swayed from side to side as the older elephant drew level with me. The animal stopped and sent a jet of yellow piss cascading onto the muddy road. The little man prodded the young elephant with a stick in an attempt to get the animals moving. A noise erupted and I was engulfed in a foul smell. Mountainous turds splattered, steaming, at my feet.

"You coming to the circus, sonny?" I didn't get a chance to answer as Mrs Morris was on the street screaming that 'the bloody Indians' were now moving 'their filthy animals in'. My mother appeared with a wheelbarrow and handed me a shovel.

"Come on, Bob; barrow this up before the neighbours see." I was just finishing my second load when the cart carrying my father arrived.

I was shocked; this was not the man I remembered. He did not leap from the cart and take my mother in his arms. Clinging to a rail with one hand, he sought the assistance of the driver with the other. His descent was faltering, that of an old man, his foot quivering a few inches above the ground, stealing himself for a safe landing. He stood, swaying slightly, a small, grubby figure staring blankly at the rectory. The driver handed him a little battered suitcase, and my mother took him by the arm and guided him gently towards the back of the house. They walked straight past me, but his face showed no sign of recognition. The curtains in the morning room were parted slightly. I could just make out the figure of Reverend Egan before abruptly he drew them, yanking at the heavy velvet drapes. Before they even reached the house my father started coughing. He stopped, wild eyes casting around. He must have known what was coming. At first just a dry hack, which orchestrated itself through a series of body-racking assaults, as if there was a volcano erupting within him. His face changed colour as the attack progressed from grey, through puce to blue. His eyes bulged and streamed. Sputum was disgorged from deep in his lungs, spraying my mother's frock. As the attack subsided, tears of impotence ran down his cheeks. I was numbed and yet strangely ashamed. Soldiers returning from war should surely cut a heroic figure. I felt someone touch my arm.

"Come," she said simply. She took my hand and I listened to the rustle of her sari as she led me to her house. Kitty was waiting at the door. I avoided her gaze, frightened I might start crying.

Kitty was dispatched to the kitchen and I was seated on an intricately carved settee. The room was strange; a mixture of dark wooden furniture covered in fabrics of wild colour and design. The furnishings – rugs, wall hangings and garish pictures – were all unlike anything I had seen in the village houses. These tended to be quite basic, with stone or linoleumed floors and an open range, which was used for cooking and heating. Even the smells of cooking here were different. Exotic spices hung on the air, intoxicating and exciting, blocking out the gloom of the English winter.

I was handed a fine china cup and saucer. I sipped. The tea tasted unusual, perfumed and heady. "Are you alright?" She had a funny, sing-song voice.

"Yes thank you, Mrs Curtis."

"Call me Sanja. I don't like 'Curtis' name." She smiled and the sadness left her face. Kitty gabbled something in a foreign tongue, giggling, only to be silenced by a ferocious look from her mother. They both fussed about me that day. It was as if they knew the trouble that was to engulf my family with the return of my father. From the beginning I felt at home in this essentially foreign house, which was often to be my refuge over the coming years. Sanja took my hand. "When you go home you must remember your daddy has had some terrible

times. Seen horrible things. Do you understand?" Her voice had a hypnotic lilt. I nodded, but I didn't really understand.
"Be kind to him, help him," she continued. "And your mother; it is a difficult time for her, too."
I nodded again. But why was it difficult? Surely she would be pleased to see him home?
"And watch out for the holy man." She squeezed my hands as she spoke.
"Holy man?" I queried.
"The Reverend." She had trouble pronouncing the word. "I don't trust that man."
"Mumma, stop it." Kitty looked embarrassed. Walking home I remembered that some villagers were referring to the Indian woman's 'devil talk'. Was she perhaps trying to fill me with heathen nonsense?
As I opened the back door to our house, I couldn't make out if it was coughing or crying I could hear coming from our small parlour.

* * * * * * * *

The visit to the Palladium turns out to be something of a disaster. They were rehearsing for a new musical due to open the next week. The show had previewed well in the provinces, but the composer had insisted on several changes, adding a new number and demanding alterations to the lyrics of two other songs. By doing so he had managed to infuriate his lyricist, director, producer, leading players and probably the whole cast. To make matters worse, the theatre management seemed to have forgotten that we were filming. We were kept waiting at the stage door until clearance was gained. A steady drizzle was falling and I complained loudly. Grumbling, our small group was led into the sparsely lit auditorium. On stage the chorus were stomping out a number, dressed incongruously as traffic wardens. In the stalls a

heated shouting match was taking place between the composer and choreographer.
"Who the bloody hell are these people?" the producer screamed. "And how, for Christ's sake, have they been let in with a camera? I gave express instructions..."
Stepping forward, Stephanie Aston explained we had been booked in for a short session. She introduced me. The music had stopped and the chorus stared down from the brightly lit stage. The composer, who had been knighted in the recent honours list, threw his score to the floor. "This is madness. We have a show to sort out and I have to play second fiddle to...who did you say?"
"Bob Mitchell – Mitch," Stephanie explained.
I held my hand out in greeting but Sir Wayne strode past me, seemingly crying into a huge red handkerchief. "OK. Take an hour," someone shouted.
A middle-aged woman apologised. "I'm so sorry, the man has no class. Not a lot of talent, either," she added.
I was introduced to George Lambert, who had apparently played tenor sax in Sydney Lipton's band at the Grosvenor House Hotel. I had played there dozens of times, but I had no recollection of George. He greets me, though, like a long-lost cousin. He is a short, spry figure, with a shock of white hair. He has either worn better than me or is some years younger. Stephanie assures me he has a number of wonderful anecdotes, which will doubtless prompt my memory. I smile. willing to go along with anything suggested. All seems well until the camera starts rolling. George, who spoke quite normally beforehand, instantly develops a dreadful stutter as soon as we go live. With each take he becomes worse, despite gentle encouragement from Stephanie. I find myself nodding in an effort to get the poor man to 'spit it out'. It is decided that I should talk first, reminding him of the old days at the Grosvenor. He chortles at my recollections, for all the world relaxed and at ease, until he is called on to reply.

"Wonderful!" He starts rubbing his hands, his face animated. "What fu, fu, fu, fu..." My God, I think to myself; what on earth is he going to say?
"Fun," he suddenly shouts out triumphantly.
Half an hour later, still very little progress has been made. The cast and chorus are returning. Stephanie is looking flustered. A white piano has been wheeled on to centre stage. She wants me to sing a number. This hasn't been mentioned. I haven't performed in public for years. I am propelled back stage and out into the bright lights. The cast applaud from below and the cameras roll. Holding on to the piano I bow.
Sixty-five years ago, I had walked onto this very stage, as top of the bill. Then I was preceded by a pretty assistant carrying the candelabra, which was carefully set on the piano. The lights were dimmed as she lit the candles. I would then kiss her gloved hand (from memory, I kissed other bits of her later), and then with my silk handkerchief I dusted the leather piano stool with a flourish. Finally, with a well-practised twirl of my tails, I would break into my version of Ray Noble's *The touch of your lips*.
Now, as I sit at the piano, I feel isolated, like a beginner at an audition. My fingers feel stiff, my throat dry. Down below angry whispers tell me that the producer and Sir Wayne Brocket have returned.
"I would like to play the number I started with when I last appeared here at the Palladium." Amazingly, my stiff old joints move effortlessly over the ivories. I sense that now I have everyone's attention. I start well enough, but my voice sounds, brittle and reedy.

The touch of your lips
Upon my brow,
Your lips that are cool and sweet,
Such tenderness lies in this soft caress
My heart forgets to beat

I have chosen a song with only two verses, but suddenly my mind is blank.
'The touch of your hand upon my head' – then what?
I improvise on the piano and return to the first verse. I hear movement below me and embarrassed coughing. I finish with a flourish, beaming at the camera. There is some polite applause. I have bombed. It has only happened to me a couple of times during a long career. On both occasions I had drunk too much before going on, depressed by half-empty theatres inhabited by audiences sheltering from foul summer seaside weather.
"Well done, that was great." Stephanie is a kind girl, but she looks worried.
"Was all that really necessary?" Sir Wayne asks no one in particular "Well, I ask you."
I am deposited back at my hotel. There is no mention of dinner with the famous Mr White – or anyone else, for that matter. I have rather let the side down.

* * * * * * * *

The war ended just a week after my father's return. Surely this was a time for great celebrations. Was everyone just too exhausted, or was it deemed poor taste to show emotion? It was a strange time; I can't even remember the church bells being rung. All the time death and injury just accepted. Life would continue to be a struggle for most people.
Recognition finally came in the form of church services the Sunday after Armistice Day. For once the whole village came together, with the Baptists attending St Helen's. The church was full to overflowing. Union Jacks were furled either side of the altar. Beresford Egan was in his element, his voice at its most sonorous. The congregation sat in strict social pecking order, which had been complicated by the attendance of the chapel-goers. Arguments and long-held resentments

came to the surface as families scrambled for what they felt was their rightful place. There was no challenging for the front pews, though, which were taken by the two most influential families in the village. To the right, the tall figure of Sir Percy Gibbs, flanked by his wife, son and senior staff. The Gibbs had lived at Theddington Hall for generations. An old-fashioned figure, Sir Percy wore a frock coat with a black armband prominent on his sleeve. His wife, Dorothy, had not been seen in public since their eldest son's death, at the first battle for Ypres. She was also dressed in black. Inconsolable on the news of her son's death, she had turned to food for consolation. The villagers now stole guilty glances at Lady Dorothy, who had bloated alarmingly and was unrecognisable from the elegant figure they remembered. At her side stood Evelyn, their youngest boy, dressed in the uniform of the Northamptonshire regiment. Taller still than his father, he cut a stylish figure, the empty sleeve for his left arm tucked under his shining Sam Browne. His eyes were never still. He kept glancing round, ill at ease. I was reminded of a caged animal. To the left stood the Champions. They lived at the other end of the village, in a burgeoning mansion, which William Champion had started building in 1911. It was set on a hill overlooking Stratton Market, where their corset factory was the town's largest employer. During the war the firm had gained valuable contracts, making webbed belts and gaiters. William's family had come from Lancashire in the mid-19th century. Starting with a single haberdashery shop, they expanded gradually into manufacturing, until currently they employed over 1,000 workers in Stratton Market alone. William was now in his mid-fifties, a coarse-looking man with thinning hair. Short and powerful in stature, the combination of his broad shoulders, sloping at an acute angle, with his short, sturdy legs gave an impression of huge physical strength. He was a man of unique business acumen and an enlightened employer for his time. There had been much muttering as to why neither of his sons has seen service during the war. Instead Fred and James dedicated themselves to ever increasing the efficiency of the Champion factories. Both, although slightly taller and with more hair, were of similar build to their father. James, the younger, had married the previous year, to the daughter of a Yorkshire mill-owner. She stood between the sons, a rather plain girl but 'well put together', as William frequently commented.

Lettice Champion, William's wife, had been a legendary beauty in her day. The daughter of an impoverished Northern Irish titled family, she had brought élan and class to complement her husband's talent for making money. Still a beautiful woman, she wore a coat of the darkest green and a wide-brimmed hat. She was a controversial character. Outlandish and eccentric, she was despised by the local gentry, but she refused to conform. She was even reputed to sit astride a horse when riding in their parkland, rather than side-saddle.

Shiny suits and best coats of sober shades were lined up in the pews behind the two grand families. Miss Ormerod stood upright like a guardsman. Widows and children who had lost their fathers listened to choir sing *Jerusalem* with quivering lips.

I could just catch sight of Kitty some three or four rows in front of us; she was holding her father's hand. Sanja was one of the few villagers not present to join in an impassioned offering of *Abide with me*.

Beside me, my mother was casting anxious glances at my dad. He was trying to draw in huge breaths, his face a deathly pallor. The singing of the hymn finished and Reverend Egan made his way slowly to the pulpit. "Bert, get some fresh air," my mother urged, but my father stood defiantly, the first dry hack sounding like gunfire in the quietened congregation.

"Dearly beloved, on this historic day..," the rector intoned. The attack now racked through my father's arched body. The

mustard gas had done its job. I felt ashamed of myself, for being ashamed of my dad. He tried to cover his mouth, but a filthy-coloured spittle seeped through his fingers. My mother tried to cradle him in her arms, but he fought her off.
"Get that man out," Beresford Egan boomed from the pulpit. My father pushed wildly passed me. All eyes were on him, many showing compassion, some outright distaste.
"When God, in his infinite mercy..," the rector continued. The attack had almost passed now and my father stood panting, staring up at the pulpit.
"Please leave us, until you have quite recovered, Mr Mitchell." The cleric's tone was dismissive. For a moment he looked as if he would obey the request. I watched my father carefully as the rector droned on.
I had been aware of the tension at home since my father's return. Beresford Egan was paranoid about noise, hence my not being able to practice on the piano when he was in the house. My father's attacks were not allowed to go uncommented on by the rector. My mother, desperate to retain her job, had promised that things would improve, but if anything the attacks were becoming worse.
My father shuffled towards the door, but then all the unfairness and indignity of what he had been through must have welled up inside him. All the pain of lost mates, shattered bodies, mud, blood and gas. For a second he seemed to regain his strength. He almost strode down the aisle, pointing as he did so. "You bastard," he roared. I felt my mother's body stiffen beside me. "You slimy sod. Some of us fought for this day. Call yourself a Christian?"
"Get him out of here!" the rector screamed, but everyone seemed too shocked to move. Beside me my mother started shaking, either from fear or mortification. He had started coughing again; I cried out in anguish. As he held onto a pew for support a figure appeared at his side.

"Come," she said, and I listened to the rustle of her sari as she supported him as they walked to the double doors and into the cold, slanting rain of a November morning.

CHAPTER 5

For a few days after my father's outburst his physical condition seemed to improve. It was as if he had somehow exorcised the mucus from his lungs. I felt proud of him. He was a man, after all. A brave, fearless man, prepared to take on the unfairness of the world as represented by the establishment. My mother's face told another story. She bore a haunted look. Like a prisoner awaiting a verdict the result of which she already knew.

Beresford Egan was too sophisticated a man to act as a direct result of my father's indiscretion. Moreover, he needed to find a replacement for my mother before passing sentence. For several days our lives continued as normal on the surface. Despite my mother's pleading, dad refused to apologise to the rector. It was if he had become liberated. For the first time since his return he played games with me. I had forgotten about his broad smile.

The two men gave each other a wide berth. It was on the following Saturday that we were given notice. Elsie Wharton, who had been widowed earlier in the year, was appointed as the vicar's new housekeeper. Reverend Egan made no mention of the furore in the church when giving my mother the terrible news. Rather, he suggested, the accommodation he was able to offer us was inadequate for three people. It would be in our own interest to move on. Besides, the additional noise made life difficult for him, particularly when he was attempting to compose inspiring sermons.

My father's health went into an immediate decline. The frightening fits of coughing launched themselves at him with increasing severity and regularity. Dad was full of rage, which only worsened his condition. In between spasms he ranted, his voice clearly heard by passers-by in the street. He reckoned he was going to give the rector "a bloody good hiding." In truth, he had hardly the strength to get out of bed.

We had nowhere to take our few possessions. My mother warned that the workhouse beckoned.
Each morning now I walked to school with Kitty, and I told her of our troubles. News spread rapidly in the village, and I was aware that Miss Ormerod was being much kinder to me than usual.
A couple of nights before we were due to leave the rectory I was woken by urgent, hushed talking below in our parlour. I strained, trying to listen. There were three or four voices, interspersed by my dad's coughing. The following morning the mood in the house was lighter. We were moving in on a temporary basis with Kitty's parents.
Beresford Egan made a great show of helping us move our few pieces of furniture, rag rugs and cooking utensils. He loaned us a handcart, to move the smaller items to Railway House. The piano and the larger pieces of furniture were transported to a shed down at Theddington station. The rector repeatedly thanked my mother for all her past work, particularly when there were neighbours around to hear his commendation. He even wished my father Godspeed and a full recovery. He was, after all, a magnanimous man. A violent fit of coughing overtook my father, and he beat at his chest in frustration. The village, though, still looked up to their rector. The consensus was that no one could behave like my father and expect to get away with it.
How long did we live at the Railway House? I really can't remember. Certainly no more than a month, although I have no recollection of having spent Christmas there. My mother wrote to our relatives in Derbyshire and applied for the few jobs advertised that she was qualified for. The Curtis family were very kind to us, but arrangements were far from ideal. My parents lived in a small spare bedroom, whilst I shared a more spacious room with Kitty. I slept on a small camp bed beside hers. We had become great friends and there was no awkwardness with the two of us living in such close

proximity. Most nights we lay together on her bed, reading or playing cards. Some nights I became vaguely aware of Sanja or my mother lifting me up and gently tucking me into my own bed. It was a fascinating time for me, unable to really understand the seriousness of our situation. No one wanted to take on my mother, with an invalid husband and a young son to look after. I, though, enjoyed the companionship of a new friend, and also the strange, spicy food that Sanja cooked for us.

Earlier in the summer the great influenza epidemic had swept through the country, leaving thousands dead. Fifty-four people had succumbed in Stratton Market. My father was possibly the last fatality of the outbreak in the area. It was Kitty's father who brought the virus into the house, although he suffered only a relatively mild form. My dad had seemed to be getting stronger until that time. He was coming downstairs regularly and taking short walks in the garden. His coughing fits were becoming less frequent and he was even talking wistfully about getting a job. With Mr Curtis almost recovered, he developed a fever one night. The doctor came. There were hushed discussions. He was nursed around the clock by my mother and Sanja. I was not allowed to see him, but I wasn't worried. I was enjoying life. Kitty was slowly being accepted at school and each night she helped with my homework.

I think it was about three days after the onset of my father's flu we returned home from school to see a cart drawn by two black horses standing outside the house. At first I didn't make any connection, just concentrating on the beauty of the horses, which were jigging between the wooden shafts and pawing the ground with their hoofs. Then I noticed a small group of neighbours huddled together. The women with their shawls gathered round their necks to ward off the cold. The men, caps in hand, scuffed their feet, as if embarrassed at letting their curiosity get the better of them. Only then I saw it. A plain wooden box resting on the back of the cart. My mother was standing on the doorstep, her head cradled to Sanja'a breast. Mr Littlejohn, the local carpenter and undertaker, bowed to the women and climbed up onto the cart next to the driver. With a flick of the reins the horses were turned in a semicircle, and slowly the cart moved towards us. There was no sound for a moment. Straw had been laid outside the house. As the cart drew level with us the wheels made contact with the road and I noticed the coffin bounce, as if my father was trying to rejoin us.

Death is difficult for a young child to comprehend. I had assumed my father would recover. Not just from the flu, but make a total recovery. I don't think I felt sorry for myself, or, at that moment, even for my father. It was to Connie that my heart went out. Seeing me now she stood arms outstretched, a feint nervous smile breaking out on her tear-stained face. As I started to run towards her Kitty took my hand. She squeezed it and it was only then that I began to cry.

* * * * * * * *

I can't stand the thought of another evening in my hotel room. "The Ritz," I tell the taxi-driver. I feel the need for a little luxury and familiarity. It's certainly still luxurious, but they have moved the gent's cloakroom. So much for familiarity. A porter directs me. Increasing visits to the lavatory are just one of the irritations with the passing of the years. Old age is a stealthy but undefeated enemy. Speed of reaction, loss of sight and hearing go in tandem. We spend more time in bed, yet sleep less. The nights are punctuated with unsettling dreams and a bursting bladder.

The sitting area and bar at the hotel have changed, but are still recognisable from the days when I entertained here. I remember particularly the heady times at the end of the war. Somehow, I still expect to see uniforms here. All three services. They tended to be mainly officers, but also attractive, well-connected girls from the code-busting centre at Bracknell, sporting not even a single stripe.

The waiter is attentive. He holds the chair as I carefully lower myself. I think he is Spanish and new to the job. His uniform is several sizes too large for him, his trousers trailing on the floor as he goes to get my Martini cocktail. It is early; there are only a few tables occupied. People stare at me, in that uninterested way that is the preserve of those staying at luxury hotels.

Have I come here to relive the past because I know it will be my last visit? As I sip at my excellent cocktail I know that it will also be my final trip to London. This conviction is absolute. I feel no sense of despair in the knowledge or one of maudlin sentimentality.

I am on my second cocktail. The tables around me are taken by a group of Japanese, burdened by shopping bags and festooned with expensive cameras. At the far end of the room a pianist has arrived. A middle-aged man with jug ears. He has started a rather desultory rendering of a selection of Lloyd Webber melodies. I am the only one who seems to have registered that he is playing. His style mirrors someone at a party who has nothing of interest to say and who would rather stay anonymous. The man has played at too many venues where he forms just a background noise. He is competent, but doesn't presume to break into the consciousness of his audience. As if in a trance, he improvises to such an extent that the melody is scarcely recognisable.

I am quite light-headed, but the pianist is annoying me. For a moment I am tempted to take over from him. I think better of it, remembering my earlier dismal performance at the Palladium.

I pay my bill, which is double what I anticipate. I am unsteady on my feet. I see a young couple step, laughing, arm in arm, into the lift. The memory crashes in on me. That ride

to the top floor. The massive luxury suite, where, outside, we had sat dangerously perched on a parapet, legs dangling, peering down on the traffic in Piccadilly and the crowds in Green Park. In the distance we were able to glimpse the walled gardens of Buckingham Palace. I remember our nervous laughter, as we hoisted ourselves onto the parapet above our balcony. The sudden look of vulnerability on her face and the overwhelming sense that the slightest slip would send us crashing onto the busy street below.
The waiter asks me if I am alright. Grunting, I gently push him away. The spell is not completely broken. Time evaporates. I can see her again, that night, as we were walked from the lift. A crowded room gradually went quiet. All eyes were on us, or – rather – her. She had tied her hair back from her face and worked it into a single pigtail, which reached the small of her back. She wore an evening gown of canary yellow that highlighted the colour of her skin. She was, quite simply, stunning.
I feel rather foolish. There are tears flowing down my cheeks. The waiter looks concerned, but is perceptive. "Memories?" he says. I nod and move slowly towards the door. The pianist is playing *The London I love*. I pause and raise a hand in his direction. He can actually play well when he sets his mind to it. I realise he has recognised me. His playing now is a tribute. He stands up and points towards me: "Ladies and gentlemen, the one and only Mitch." The tourists and businessmen look on in curiosity, but the pianist is the only one to applaud. I feel strangely touched. The commissionaire hails a taxi. I tip him far too generously. Why do I still want people to think well of me? And why now am I pursuing a ghost?

* * * * * * * *

The reverend Beresford Egan conducted my father's funeral service. I imagined him lying cold and still in his coffin, yet furious at having to endure the vicar's insincere tributes. He was, we were told, a man who had given his life for his country. The influenza, a mere-by-product of the suffering he had endured at Mons, Arras and Ypres.
There were only a handful of people at the graveside as his body was lowered into the damp clay. A cold wind blew in from the east, and rain that threatened to turn to sleet lashed at our faces. I remember the sad toll of the church bell. The rector seemed indifferent to the weather. He looked almost happy. He had been seen to give my father 'a good send-off'.
Kitty's mother didn't attend the service, staying at home to organise warm drinks and refreshments. She helped my mother out of her sodden coat. Poor Connie; she looked quite frail, but composed. I think she was being brave for my sake.
Sanja took my mother by the hand. "Remember, time is circular," she said. Connie looked perplexed. "Each of us has a single soul. You will meet your husband again." When I asked my mum to explain what Sanja meant that evening, she dismissed it as 'mumbo-jumbo'.
The following morning there was a knock at the door and into the living room strode Mrs Lettice Champion. "Can I have a word?" She had retained her Irish accent. Taking my mother by the arm she led her to the far side of the room. I saw Connie's face colour, and she ran a hand nervously through her hair. I was frightened that she was being given more bad news, but she took the older woman's hand and kissed it. "Thank you, thank you," she kept repeating. Mrs Champion smiled. "Come down to the house tomorrow and I'll have someone show you your quarters. I suggest you move in over the weekend."
Imperiously now she turned her attention to the rest of the room. "What a pretty child; how old is she?"
"I'm seven," Kitty replied, before her mother could answer.

Mrs Champion ignored her. "And how are you settling in, Mrs Curtis?"
"Quite well, thank you."
"Miserable lot, the English, on the whole. Make you as welcome as a drunkard at a temperance gathering," she laughed. I thought she was wonderful, but frightening. She had huge self-confidence and a throw-away irreverence that appealed. Her grey eyes now bore down on me. "What do they call you?"
"Bob, madam."
"Well, young Bob, I hope you and your mammy will be very happy living with us."
And we were!

* * * * * * * *

Within a couple of months of our arrival at Champion House my mother was promoted to the role of housekeeper. This entitled her to two rooms on the top floor of the main house. She elected to stay in the quarters we had been allocated on our arrival, however. The two small rooms were over the main arched entrance to the impressive stable block. Formed in a quadrangle, the boxes were immaculate, each with a mounting block outside. I grew up surrounded by the warmth of fresh hay and the sound and smell of horses. Our windows, which had to be removed so that our piano could be hoisted up into the living room, faced away from the house and over the walled vegetable garden. The piano rather dominated the room, but with our few pieces of furniture it was transformed into a welcoming home. Water was drawn from a pump in the yard and all food was served in the servants' hall in the main house. For several years I shared the small bedroom with my mother. Well into my teens, this arrangement was obviously no longer satisfactory. My mother took a bedroom over in the

staff quarters, and by the time I left school I had in effect my own apartment.
Mrs Champion was happy for Kitty to come and play with me after we moved in. We had great fun exploring the grounds and gardens. Nowhere was put out of bounds. I had thought the vicarage was grand, in a somewhat sombre way, but the interior of Champion House was breathtaking. The initial impression was of brightly coloured fabrics and the latest design in furniture. The ceilings were high, and massive windows gave a feeling of light, in contrast to most of the local houses. Lettice Champion was a restless spirit with an unerring eye for good design. Over the years she drew artists, writers and musicians to the house. Her tastes were considered to be attention-seeking and dubious by the local gentry. They felt more at home surrounded by paintings of their animals, family portraits and furniture handed down through generations. The interior of Champion House was quite avant-garde and dismissed by some as the downright common. My mother told me that some of the bedrooms contained shocking paintings, which I subsequently discovered were by Aubrey Beardsley and a young, little-known Eric Gill.
Rooms were constantly being redecorated and furnishings replaced. Liberty's would send up consignments on approval. It was seldom that at least part of the house was not being altered, redecorated or added to. William Champion would arrive home on many evenings to find the house in a state of changing chaos. Far from resenting this, he appeared to revel in the muddle. His wife remained to him as fascinating as the day he had first seen her walking with her father along the streets of Derry. They complimented each other. He had rescued her from a family having to endure very reduced circumstances. She had given his life meaning and a reason to strive still harder for success.

The house had been relatively small when it was built in the year I was born. Over the next 20 years it was constantly extended. Approached down a tree-lined gravel drive, the frontage was dominated by stained glass windows designed by Philip Webb. To the rear terraces had been built on three levels. On a fine summer's evening William would sit nursing a glass of good claret and look down to Stratton Market in the distance. Without shifting from his chair he could make out the solid lines of his factory in the centre of town, next to the ancient All Saints church. Business continued to expand after the war, with new export markets opening up. He joked that he made the money and his wife spent it. This was not said by way of complaint, but with pride.

Lettice Champion was an irrepressible, unpredictable bundle of energy, quite oblivious to what anyone thought of her. A true eccentric, given to wearing the most outlandish clothes. She outraged local society by wearing trousers around the village. As an employer she was difficult, given to constantly changing moods and capable of frightening rages. Over the years I came to the conclusion that much of her behaviour was designed to confuse. To keep friends on their toes and those critical of her wary. It was obvious to me, though, even as a young boy, that she had a real warmth and compassion, but she was never going to let any of us take her for granted.

I think it was during our first summer at Champion House that I was practising on the piano one afternoon. It was a sultry day and the windows were open. I was running through some of the pieces I had memorised, light classical works and popular songs of the time. I paused, deciding what to play next, when I became aware of someone in the courtyard outside.

"Is that you, young Bob?" She sounded angry. She was seated on a bay colt she had just brought over from Ireland.

"Yes, madam," I replied, moving over to the window, my colour rising in embarrassment.
"That was a great piece of playing, lad. I'm sorry you stopped."
I had no idea how long she had been listening.
"I didn't know you were so talented. When did you learn to read music?"
The horse was getting restless, jigging from side to side and throwing its head back. She sat astride the colt quite still. She was wearing a pair of men's baggy jodhpurs.
"I can't, madam."
"Good God; how do you play like that, then?"
"I don't know. Sort of from memory, I suppose."
"Well, you must have lessons. Think how good you will be then. Don't you agree?"
She didn't wait for, or probably expect, a reply. Kicking her right leg over the horse's head she dropped deftly to the ground, handing the reins to an old groom. I watched her walk up the path to the house, her thick hair of a similar colour to the two huge Irish wolfhounds that bounded over to greet her.
It is in such moments that the course of our lives changes.

CHAPTER 6

When I was a child I was told that dreams come in colour, whilst nightmares are in stark black and white. Unnervingly this is in colour, but I am awake and alert, yet unable to relegate the image from my mind.
I am playing at the Café de Paris. The diners look down on me from the balcony, whilst the floor is full of gliding dancers. The women in expensive gowns, bedecked with jewellery. The men with slicked-down hair and elegant in their tailed suits. I feel happy and, although I sense myself singing to my own accompaniment, there is no noise. Total silence, the swaying dancers occasionally offering a smile as they swing by.
The dancers part and she is walking towards me, from the far side of the room. She is radiant. She is wearing a sari in varying shades of orange. Even now my heart skips a beat. I am enveloped in a feeling of love and warmth. Only now do I notice she is holding the hand of a man whose face remains indistinct. I continue playing and they dance towards me. There is applause from the gallery. I can see the hands clapping, but no sound. He is strangely dressed, all in black. The garment reaches his shoes and is secured round his waist by a thick leather belt. At his neck he wears the collar of a cleric. They reach the piano and the other dancers continue to the beat of the silent music. With the flourish of a magician he releases the fabric of her skirt and tosses it onto a nearby table. She is naked from the waist down. I continue playing. The man hoists his cassock and exposes himself for all to see. She arches her back into the curve of the grand piano and roughly he enters her. I can feel the piano move with each thrust. A fringe of hair secured by a diamond clip breaks loose and flops rhythmically against her forehead. She turns to me. I remember that look; it's one of ecstasy. Suddenly there is sound. "Yes," she says, "yes, yes." The dancers

continue, the diners applaud. There are cheers and wolf whistles and I am singing.

It's not the pale moon that excites me
And thrills and delights me,
Oh no, it's just the nearness of you

* * * * * * * *

I hate these visions and don't understand them. I suppose it's my own fault. For years I have cut memories of Kitty from my mind, but now I am seeking her, trying again to understand what went wrong. I am unable to forget her face, mocking me, and yet I must continue.

The porter has remembered the tapes. They are neatly stacked on my dressing table. My probing into the past will continue in tandem with the programme, which like most documentaries only scratches the surface of the subject it is covering.

Last night I ate at the Criterion. Although there were queues waiting and I hadn't booked, I was ushered through. I don't think the head waiter recognised me. I do look frail and he was probably worried that I might pass out in the entrance. Illness of customers in restaurants is very disruptive; death a huge embarrassment. It happened several times during my career. "Had one too many," was the usual explanation as the body was carried out. This never quite explained the distraught wife who followed on, whilst the maître d' at her elbow tried to get the poor woman to settle the bill.

Some of the old mosaics in the restaurant have survived from before the war, but even with the tall potted palms the place fails to capture the spirit of the thirties. The food is well presented, though, and the service friendly but not intrusive. The clientele of modern restaurants fascinate me. Most are very young and yet the place is expensive. These do not appear to be the sons and daughters of inherited wealth. Their table manners would not pass muster in the officer's mess or wardroom. It seems to me they are the thrusting, confident generation who are making it on their own. Earning big money and pumping some of it straight back into the economy.

By the time I leave the restaurant it is late and the night is cold and misty. Still, crowds of youngsters throng round Piccadilly Circus. For the first time in years I feel a touch of envy. Their enjoyment is different from when I was young. There are far fewer rules about etiquette and dress, but they retain the enthusiasm of youth. Not for them looking back, as the elderly do. They travel forward with confidence to embrace their fast-changing world. As I make my way slowly the short distance back to my hotel, I don't feel threatened by these boisterous youngsters. Several stand back to allow me to pass. "You alright, mate?" they enquire, and I assure them I am.

* * * * * * * *

Miss Langley turned out to be an inspirational piano teacher. Kind yet demanding, she appreciated the natural talent I had, nurturing and constantly developing it. Youngsters are always very bad at guessing adults' ages. Anyone over 25 seemed ancient, and so it was that I assumed Miss Langley was distinctly middle-aged. Looking back, I realise that she was probably only in her late twenties. She had been engaged before the war to a schoolmaster from Stratton Market. I remember his face looking down at me from the top of the piano, in her mother's house, next to the wheelwright's yard. He had soft brown eyes and a kind expression. His eyes could have been of any colour, but the sepia photograph dictated they be brown. He had been commissioned, much to his fiancée's pride, but in so doing he had probably accelerated his own death. The mortality rate amongst junior officers far exceeded that of their men. He survived no more than three months, falling in a field just outside Béthune. Blown to pieces by a mortar shell, his only recognition was to be listed with over 200 others, on Stratton Market's war memorial, when it was unveiled in September 1921. I can only imagine the torment his death caused my teacher. To my knowledge she never had any other romantic association. She had promised herself to her fiancé and death in no way weakened this pledge. Today this reaction would be considered madness by most people, and yet to me, at the time, it showed a deep sense of true romance. She remained faithful to him and his memory. She devoted her energies to teaching pupils of varying talents the disciplines and joy of being able to play the piano. She encouraged and cajoled me into thinking that here might be an escape route from rural poverty. I understand that she took much satisfaction from my later success. Each year she sent me a Christmas card, with a chatty personal note. To my eternal shame, I seldom responded, too taken up with my own life. Now, though, I remember her rather sad, blue eyes, urging, willing me on through a particularly difficult piece. Very rarely, she would throw a tantrum when she felt my concentration or commitment was lacking. More likely it was due to her having to constantly care for her sick mother. Later she also suffered a long and distressing illness, before she died in 1967. She had become a recluse during her latter years. She had been dead for several days before her body was even discovered. The house was filthy and contained no food. One photograph album and a scrapbook were found amongst the debris. The one containing photographs of me as a boy, the other newspaper cuttings of my rise to stardom. On the piano her brown-eyed fiancé continued to look down, his face partly obliterated now by dust.

Evelyn Gibbs was another victim of the war. The loss of an arm is surely devastating for an active young man, but it was

his mind that had suffered most. I never thought of him as being mad in the accepted sense, but his experiences had left him fragile and at odds with the world. My father had served in the same regiment, although not directly under the young captain. I was never sure if it was that, or out of some sense of solidarity with my father's outburst in the church, that led him to befriend me. In fact it was Kitty who was first given access to the hall by him, and initially I just tagged along. He treated us as equals. He was childlike himself, in his enthusiasm for constant activity. It was as if, by being continually busy, he was blocking out devils that invaded his mind in times of contemplation. The hall was normally completely out of bounds to the villagers, except those who worked there. Neither did he show any interest in any other youngsters. At first we were nervous in his company and there was much talk behind our backs. I think my mother and Kitty's parents were also concerned, but found it difficult to explain why we shouldn't spend so much time with our new friend. I noticed that Evelyn tended to avoid adult male company. It was as if he had been thrown into too much close proximity with them during his time in the trenches. He was aloof and uncomfortable in their presence. He was also rude and dismissive to staff, and yet to us he was kind, friendly and amusing. The only adult he seemed to value was his mother. We tried to keep out of her way. She had a booming voice that suited her considerable bulk. She had the uncomfortable habit of talking to her son as if we weren't present.
"Evelyn, darling, what are these village children doing here? Can't you find friends of your own age? I swear that child has a touch of the tar brush!" So she would go on. He would also reply as if we didn't exist. "They amuse me, mother. Who else is there round here?" He would quickly become agitated and Lady Dorothy would go into reverse.
"As you wish, darling. Don't upset yourself. You know best."

The Gibbs' estate extended to some 2,000 acres. Sir Percy spent much of his time abroad. There was dark talk of a 'fancy woman' in London. I never knew Evelyn to do a day's work. He was, after all, a gentleman. I have no idea where the money came from to sustain the large staff they employed. Presumably they had investments in some commercial projects, which produced income in addition to their tenant farms. To them and their like, trade was considered a dirty word.

When Evelyn first showed us round the gardens and then the house, the staff were unable to conceal their amazement. We were even served tea in the drawing room. Although Evelyn knew where I lived, the Champions were never mentioned. The hall was much larger than Champion House. Drab by comparison, but somehow grander. The living rooms were vast with massive marble fireplaces, above which hung ornate gilded mirrors, giving the impression of still more space. Antique furniture glowed under years of constant polishing. Intimidating family portraits, of men in uniform and haughty-looking dowagers stared down. In summer the house remained dark and cold. It came to life only in winter, when logs gathered from the estate were thrown onto fires, casting weird shadows and gradually warming the fabric of the building.

Outside in the gardens it was possible to see why the English gained a reputation for eccentricity. Sir Percy had been a keen cricketer in his youth. He had played for the county, for a couple of seasons. Some 50 years beforehand a cricket pitch and outfield had been laid, adjoining the west wing. For years Test and county players had taken part in a week-long cricket festival, held each September. Although this event had ceased years ago, the cricket field remained. The square was still regularly prepared with two giant carthorses, their feet encased in mufflers, drawing the heavy iron roller behind them. There was also a seven-hole golf course, complete with deep bunkers. This was used only by Evelyn, who before the war had a low handicap. He still managed to hit the ball good distances and with great accuracy. Often Kitty accompanied him, and as I grew older I acted as his caddy. Although he was still a better-than-average player, his disability annoyed him and he was liable to work himself up into a rage. He would throw his clubs on the ground and storm off, leaving us to collect them, to be safely stowed in the scullery.

Kitty seemed happier wandering around the hall grounds rather than at Champion House. So it was that I spent several of my holidays staying with her parents. With the passing of time one holiday merges with another. Our pleasures were simple. We picked fruit, climbed trees and went sledging when the snow came. Evelyn was quite fearless, inviting danger by choosing icy roads on the estate rather than snowy fields. I can remember his cries of elation, as he hurtled down the hill drive leading towards the staff quarters.

Although I had lived in the village all my life, Kitty seemed to know of places in the surrounding fields that I had never discovered. Derelict farm buildings hidden by undergrowth, an abandoned tree house on the edge of Theddington woods. It was she who first discovered the ice store, down a narrow lane in a valley out of sight of the house, situated on a north-facing slope. We inched our way gingerly down steps made from railway sleepers. Pushing the door open we left the warm summer sunshine behind and, peering through the gloom, looked in awe at the giant slabs of ice. We shivered as we touched them before, becoming braver, we licked the ice, so cold that for a moment it seemed our tongues would become stuck.

Kitty was the leader and I happily followed, wondering what new hiding place or den she would discover. "Come on," she said, "the crab apples will be ready in the orchard." It wasn't long since we had been given the run of the grounds. I followed her through the huge vegetable garden, with its endless rows of greenhouses. There must have been about a dozen men working, digging, hoeing and a couple throwing barrow loads of weeds onto a smouldering bonfire. Kitty stopped. “Come on, get a move on,” I called. Half turning her back, she ran past the fire, ignoring the backchat from a young lad who stood grinning at us, pitchfork in hand. Kitty wiped her eyes as the smoke continued to billow towards us. She broke into a trot. “Quick, this way; there’s a door we can get through.” She stopped suddenly, staring ahead. She looked confused.

“What do you think you two are up to, then?” Mr Armstrong, the head gardener, had worked at the hall all his life. He imposed an iron discipline over his staff. He was old, old-fashioned and grumpy. A frightening figure in a frock coat, coarse trousers, top hat and white gloves. We knew he couldn’t understand why Mr Evelyn had given two urchins the run of the place. He was responsible for overseeing all work in the gardens. He moved stealthily around his territory, appearing when least expected. “Weed!” he would shout, pointing accusingly with a gloved hand, as one of his gardeners scrambled to remove the source of his irritation.

“We were trying to get through to the orchard,” Kitty said. I could see the outline of the old doorway, blocked with large, modern bricks.

“Orchard?” He seemed quite cross at the suggestion. “There’s no orchard here. Them’s were cut down 30 years since. Now, scram!”

CHAPTER 7

I was always uneasy sleeping in the bed where my father had died. Kitty's parents were always welcoming, but I never really liked staying overnight. The bedroom overlooked the graveyard, where his remains lay. I would lie awake for hours, waiting for a reluctant sleep to overcome me. My childish mind imagined my father rising from his grave and appearing at my bedside. The lamp in my room burnt all night, hoping this would dissuade him. My mother rarely mentioned him now. I felt uncomfortable with his memory. Despite his war record, I was aware that he was thought to have rather let himself down, and by default some of the blame had attached itself to me. Whereas the upper classes were expected to show a stiff upper lip, those lower down the social scale were similarly required to accept whatever misfortune was heaped upon them without complaint.

It had been assumed that the end of the war would bring better times. The reverse was true. Only the Champions appeared to prosper. By the beginning of the twenties, fashions mirrored the massive changes in society. Pinched-in waists became fashionable and corsets were in decline. The modern, emancipated women sought freedom and a less formal appearance. The flat 'flapper' look arrived. As ever, William anticipated the change. The manufacture of traditional corsets was cut back. Demand for bandeaux was phenomenal worldwide. The garment flattened the bust, some being secured by the new innovation of hook and eye fastenings. Liberty bodices were also introduced, which allowed freedom of movement whilst supporting the figure. Two new factories were set up south of Stratton Market to accommodate the increased demand, and Fred, or Mr Frederick, as he was now known, took over the running of the new plants. He purchased a Victorian mansion set in some 200 acres within a couple of miles of the new factories. His younger brother,

James, moved to London with his wife to take charge of the impressive showrooms and sales department on Sloane Street.
Most of the villagers, other than those employed by the Champions, were struggling. The pound had lost over half of its value from pre-war levels, while death duties levied at 40% ensured that huge tracts of land changed hands. Great estates were broken up and acquired by industrialists. Many landowners retrenched in smaller houses. Some even deserted the shires entirely, favouring their homes in Knightsbridge and Kensington.
Unemployment rose with the return of the troops from around the world. Many found that their jobs had been taken by women, who were more productive and cheaper to employ. Young women sought factory work, no longer willing to go into service, with its poor pay, long hours and back-breaking duties. On the land conditions were even worse. Free trade led to an influx of imports. The price for cattle and sheep collapsed and much of the land lay untouched and covered in weeds. In Stratton Market a chain of national grocers arrived, leading to the closure of several small shops. Many pondered as to whether the massive sacrifice made during the war had been worthwhile.
My mother was content enough. Some of the 'Champion magic' attached itself to those who worked for them. The company provided superb facilities for its staff in Stratton Market. There was a splendid sports field with adjoining tennis courts. A social club ran regular weekend dances and served drinks at virtually half the price of the local pubs. A motorbus was laid on each Saturday, and Connie, a keen dancer, would go whenever she had the night off. The company even employed a full-time nurse, and Lettice Champion would make a point of serving teas in the clubhouse at least once a week. Were the Champions genuinely interested in their employees' well-being? I don't honestly know, but they were years ahead of their time in the

facilities they offered. Perhaps the whole family were just brilliant entrepreneurs. They had a waiting list for those wanting to join the company. William expected a full day's work from all his staff, but it was a brilliant format, which took generations to falter.
Lettice Champion now sought my mother's advice on the ever-changing internal decor in the house. Perhaps 'advice' is too strong a word – more like 'agreement' – but Connie loved the never-ending lengths of fabric and wallpapers to be pored over. Pale almond, green and grey, with just a touch of yellow, now dominated the major living rooms. Simplicity was the latest watchword, nothing fussy or too ornamental, and gradually our own living quarters became full of cloisonné bowls, ivory carvings and garish Egyptian wall hangings. Lettice Champion never sold anything she no longer liked. Important items were given to family or friends. Articles she thought of little consequence were distributed amongst the staff.
During this period my life was a constant round of school and piano lessons interspersed with holidays, which were looked forward to with huge anticipation. By now I was a firm favourite of Miss Ormerod, playing the piano each morning at assembly. My recitals for visiting inspectors became longer and more impressive with the passing of each year. Kitty showed the most amazing capacity for absorbing facts. She was already more than a year ahead of most of her contemporaries. This could have led to her being very unpopular with the other pupils, but she was also cheeky and had a happy knack of being able to defuse Miss Ormerod when she ranted and raved. We both had other friends, but during holidays we were inseparable.
It must have been at least three years after my father died that I was staying at Kitty's house towards the end of the summer holiday. I had fallen asleep covered only by a sheet, having become very hot playing football on the green. Five or six of

us had tackled furiously before shooting at Kitty, who was keeping goal between two piles of discarded sweaters. She had become a real tomboy and was a very acrobatic goalkeeper. The nights were becoming chilly and I can remember reaching out to pull the blankets round me. I'm not sure if it was a noise or the flickering light that woke me. Peeping through the curtains I could make out two vague figures amongst the gravestones. I was petrified. Ghosts did exist! A man was holding a lamp and in its shadow a young, ghost-like figure clutched a small box to her breast. A discarded spade lay on a mound of freshly dug earth. I imagined the figures had risen from the grave. The young woman knelt and lowered the box into the earth. Standing, she read from a small prayer book, the man holding the wavering lamp above her head. Suddenly there were more lights and shouting and cursing, and punches were thrown. The woman screamed. An eerie wail shattering the stillness of the night. The man was wrestled to the ground, struggling and shouting abuse.

Mr Curtis came in and ordered me back to bed. Some time later Kitty sneaked into bed with me. She was cold and bony. I tried to frighten her with some unlikely ghost stories. She became quite angry, elbowing me in the ribs. She was already frightened and told me not to joke about such things. Rolling over, she went straight to sleep. It was comfortable feeling her warmth against me. When I woke, she was holding my hand. I didn't move. I felt very protective towards my best friend. For the first time I wanted to cuddle her, but I knew she would think I was being silly.

The adults in the village tried to draw a veil of secrecy over what had happened in the churchyard. Preposterous rumours swept through the school playground. It was only a snippet in the local paper that revealed the truth. Nancy Baldwin, a scullery maid at the hall, had become pregnant and had managed to disguise her condition with the help of a

Champion corset. The child had been delivered with the help of Agnes Plowman, another maid at the hall. At her trial Nancy insisted the child had been stillborn, but being a devout Christian she had been determined to give the baby a Christian burial. Enoch Salmon, a junior gardener, had agreed to help by digging the grave. Placing the child in a shoebox Nancy proceeded to conduct her child's funeral service. Unfortunately for her someone at the house informed Lady Dorothy, and Ted Margeston, the local constable, lay in wait for them with two helpers. Enoch Salmon denied being the father but was imprisoned at the assizes, along with Nancy, who was found guilty of infanticide; Agnes Plowman was dismissed without a reference.

Right into adulthood I remained frightened of the dark; I was already haunted by an earlier incident in my childhood. We were still living at the rectory when, one night, there was a noise of clattering milk bottles outside our door. Having gone to investigate, my mother returned supporting a filthy, wide-eyed young man. He spoke with an accent that I couldn't understand. I cowered, frightened at the way he tore at the food my mother gave him and spilled the water in his urgency to gulp it down. I was sworn to secrecy as Connie sent the young man on his way, with two rounds of cheese sandwiches and a slab of fruit cake. We learnt the following day that he was picked up just outside Leicester by the military police. He was heading for Newcastle in an attempt to win back his wife, who had taken up with a commercial traveller. He had been on the run for a month. He never did see his wife. He was shipped back to his regiment in Belgium for court martial. Found guilty of desertion he was shot, tied to a stake on an early December morning in a wet courtyard in Popperinge. We learnt early in those days that wrongdoings were severely punished.

* * * * * * * *

I must have slept awkwardly. I have pins and needles in my arm. I feel quite well, though, and I am looking forward to today. We are visiting the house where I lived when I first came to London. What an exciting and happy time! Then, in the afternoon, the programme editor is showing me all the film clips that she has been able to find of me performing. Some go back to my very earliest appearances and she hopes I will be able to remember dates and venues.
I breakfast early in my room. I can't face jostling with all those tourists again. The kippers are first-class. We were due to travel up to the Midlands tonight, but selfishly I have insisted I shall be too tired. A little of the star temperament still asserting itself. We will travel up by train in the morning. Stephanie has asked me to join her and her partner for dinner. I accepted. I quite like her. She is very professional and efficient, but underneath I sense a kind soul seeking a little love and affection. Perhaps she should be married and have children. Career women seem to sacrifice so much.

* * * * * * * *

I discovered the boating lake in the woods almost by chance. Kitty and I had spent hours playing in the hall grounds, but she always insisted she was too frightened to venture far into the wooded area. This started beyond the water meadow, on a hill to the east of the hall. The woods were particularly beautiful in the spring, when the whole area was carpeted in bluebells. I had just had one of my rare rows with Kitty. I was staying at her house and she had been intent on revising for an exam, which was coming up immediately we returned to school. It was a lovely sunny day at the end of the summer holidays and the last thing I wanted to think about was school. She could be pathetic sometimes!
Trudging up the High Street I was passed by Mr Champion in his chauffeur-driven Humber. The peace of the village was

regularly being interrupted now by motor vehicles. The previous week a lorry had crashed into the church wall, much to the vicar's annoyance. Following the mulched path I ventured further into the woods than I had ever done before. The tall trees blotted out the sun and I felt quite cold. My legs brushed against ferns and tangled undergrowth. All around birds sang me on my way. After a while the path petered out. Treading carefully through a thick clump of nettles, I came across a clearing that sloped down to the water's edge. A pair of swans across the lake viewed me warily, flanked by their young. Closer by a group of ducks squawked in alarm. This was a magical spot, quite cut off from the rest of the world. Completely surrounded by trees, the only noise was of birdsong and the gentle ripple of water as the ducks made their way across the lake, escaping from a rare human intruder. Almost hidden under the shadow of giant beech trees was the boathouse. The building jutting out over the water and, supported on stilts, it looked neglected and forlorn. The paintwork to the clapboard exterior was peeling and many of the railings to the balcony were broken. It was just possible to make out a terraced area to the side of the jetty, overgrown now with weeds. Climbing up the rotting steps I cupped my hands and peered through the smeared and cobwebbed windows. I could make out furniture dotted about the room and pictures on the wall. As I turned the handle to the door, two wood pigeons flapped noisily from a neighbouring tree, crying in alarm. I froze. I felt I was being watched. I waited. No sound, nothing moved. The door appeared to be locked. I pushed and the door, grudgingly, gave a little. I looked around, still not convinced I was alone. No, it was just a feeling of guilt. I knew that, if I was found trying to break in, I would be in trouble. I was trespassing. I put my shoulder to the door and, pushing harder, I turned the handle.

The door gave and I stumbled into a large, dusty room. There was a strange stillness to the air and a smell of age, as if oxygen had been denied access for years. I coughed, trying to clear the dust from my lungs. Old Persian rugs lay on the boarded floor and two old-fashioned loungers on rollers faced a picture window overlooking the lake. The fabric of two large settees, were faded and eaten away by mice. A table was set for tea, the crockery and the teapot covered in cobwebs and mice droppings. To the right of the door onto the balcony a huge brass telescope was mounted onto a substantial tripod. Tentatively I peered through the glass. I picked up the swans in giant relief. Gently swinging the instrument round and upwards, I was able to follow the swallows as they swooped low over the water before careering skywards. I could pick out every tree in sharp contrast, even the veins on their leaves.

I was excited. What an amazing place, and yet the atmosphere was oppressive. A newspaper lay at the side of one of the lounging chairs. Darkened with age, it was framed in sharp relief by the dusty floorboards that surrounded it. I was drawn to an old photograph on the wall. A solemn group of bewhiskered gentlemen and ladies in bustled gowns stare down from the main entrance to the hall. In the foreground the hunt gathers, a mêlée of top hats, hunting coats and top-hatted ladies sitting side-saddle.

There was a small galley kitchen off the main room. I recoiled. Flies and bluebottles covered the surfaces. The roof was damaged. It was possible to see daylight. A light breeze only accentuated the sweet, rancid smell that clogged my nostrils.

Urgently needing some fresh air, I turned the rusty key to the door opening onto the balcony. Most of the railings were rotting or had disappeared, but the steps down to the jetty were sound. The sun was high in the sky now, and although there was a film of weed near to the shore the water looked inviting. I was a competent swimmer, although not as good as Kitty. Pulling down my braces, I slipped out of my trousers and woollen shirt. The sun was warm on my skin. I listened carefully, worried still that I was being watched. The only sounds were of an English summer. Gratefully, I slipped into the cool lake. Ducking under the weed the water was clear, but it tasted brackish. Keeping an eye out for the swans I swam slowly to the shore, using a steady breaststroke. Clambering out I threw some stones, skidding them across the water. I thought I saw the bushes on the far bank move. Again I had the feeling I was being watched. I felt uneasy, rather than frightened. The swans had swum across the lake now and had positioned themselves outside the boathouse. Dutifully they watched as the cygnets dived amongst the weeds and algae. I had no alternative but to make my way round the edge of the lake, trying to avoid the nettles and brambles. Crows cawed mournfully above me. My legs were badly stung and my shoulders felt prickly from the sun. When I came to a clear stretch I ran, feeling quite liberated without any constricting clothes.

At last I reached the jetty. I stared in horror. My clothes were gone. I had left them on the jetty neatly folded with my boots on top. I ran around peering into the surrounding undergrowth. Nothing. Panic; how could I go back to Kitty's house naked? The long walk through the hall gardens. The trek down the High Street. It was impossible.

I ran up the stairs, slamming the door behind me. I needed time to think. I was frightened now. I stumbled over my boots. Instinctively I grabbled the telescope for support and saw my clothes, still neatly folded on one of the dusty lounging chairs. The relief was colossal. As I buttoned my shirt, I saw something glinting on the bank nearest the hall. I swung the telescope round. Someone was crouching in the undergrowth. A pair of binoculars were pointed my way. He sensed he had been spotted and, turning, darted into the cover of the trees. It was a figure I knew. I was worried and

confused. Hurriedly I finished dressing; I was certain now that I was going to be in big trouble.
Locking the door onto the balcony I turned and noticed another photograph hanging next to the entrance. I really wanted to be out and on my way home as soon as possible, but there was something in the photograph that caught my attention. Just a fleeting glimpse that stopped me in my tracks.
The photograph was of a group, taken – presumably – on a boat trip from the lake, looking back to the boathouse. The building appeared new. No peeling paintwork or damaged roof. Ladies in crinolined gowns and gentlemen in frock coats, some wearing stove-pipe hats, take tea on the terrace. Standing on the balcony an old man with grey hair and a bushy white beard stares down from across the years. Next to him a stout lady with a haughty look glances almost accusingly at her guests on the terrace. Seated and partly obscured by the balcony rails is an exotic figure, somehow at odds with the formal setting. Her hair is loose around her face. It is as if she is reluctant to be a participant in having this scene recorded. She is looking away from the camera, but I recognise her as the Indian woman captured in the painting we discovered at the rectory. Standing furthest from her another face smiles directly at the camera. This is a handsome face, with an aquiline nose, good jaw and full fleshy lips. His wavy hair reaches the collar of his strange, flowing gown. Around his neck hangs a huge pewter crucifix.

CHAPTER 8

I am standing opposite the building in Frith Street where I lived when I first came to London in 1931. As the cameras roll I have a catch in my voice. I wipe a tear from my eye. I feel very emotional, and yet I was happy here all those years ago. My moods are strange. There is a new sense of vulnerability about me and yet no one here can comfort me. My age forms a chasm about me. To the young people involved with the programme I am just another job. Next week a new project. The sad old performer forgotten, until the programme is shown. Then a bout of self-congratulation, the hope of good reviews in the nationals, and I am consigned to history. That I don't mind, but they patronise me. I am upset and they don't know why. Neither do I. I think they like my breakdown. It helps make good television. Eventually they stop filming and allow me to compose myself. The building looks very much the same, except that the old brickwork has been covered with a white rendering, which is beginning to peel. The premises are occupied now by a rather seedy restaurant. Surrounded by good and famous competitors, with whom they can't compete, they have failed to find a satisfactory niche. They occupy that difficult middle ground, above the fast food joints but not offering anything much in addition. An illegal immigrant chef serves up indifferent dishes from the cheapest produce. People who eat here will generally not return. They rely on downmarket tourists and visitors from the provinces on a tight budget.

We are filmed in the basement, surrounded by catering packs of cooking oil, rice and pasta. The owner is agitated and we struggle to find an area that is clean and looks reasonable. It was in this small room that I spent hours with 'Fat Man' Filkins. Long sessions playing blues, honky-tonks and ballads. Sometimes just chords repeated endlessly and others

given over to improvisation, and occasionally, when the feeling took him, we reverted to classical pieces.
My old room on the top floor is occupied by a young stockbroker. The steep stairs are carpeted now, but they take their toll. My breath comes in short gasps. For a moment I am quite light-headed. Did I really spend two years of my life here? The room is spotless, the furnishings aggressively modern. A huge television and two computer screens dominate. I cast my mind back to the flimsy furniture, linoleumed floor and gas lamps that were still in use then.
It had been my first visit to London. In fact my first venture out of my home county. Arriving at St Pancras I was overwhelmed by the noise and bustle even before I left the station. The hissing of the huge locomotives, the cries of newspaper-sellers. Everyone seemed to be rushing. The girls looked so sophisticated, the older women frightening. The men swaggered or loitered, soon to be swallowed up by another swarm of people. Cloth caps, bowlers, homburgs, pulled down trilbies, twirled umbrellas, thin roll-your-own cigarettes. Everyone seemed to project the background they came from, or – perhaps – just where they aspired to be. Huge red buses, some open-topped, roared and growled, picking their way through the clanging trams. There were more cars than I had seen in a lifetime. Hooters sounded. The smell from hundreds of exhausts filled my lungs. There were shoeshine boys, gypsies selling violets from wicker baskets. I tried to stop people to ask them where I was to catch my bus. I'm sure they just pointed me in the first direction that came into their heads, hardly pausing before rushing on to be gobbled up by the crowds that packed the pavements.
Eventually I caught the right bus. I felt everyone was looking at me. Was it my accent or my clothes? At home my suit was reckoned to be smart. Here the heavy tweed felt old-fashioned and out of place. As we travelled towards the West End the shops became smarter. Massive stores like palaces,

their windows crammed with everything that was desirable. Stop, start, revving engines, and all the way along the route crowds of people thronged the pavements. Young women with figures like boys, in short skirts. Nannies in uniform, pushing unwieldy black prams. Two sailors ejected onto the street, from a pub in Tottenham Court Road. An organ-grinder, with a monkey on a chain. A band of ex-servicemen walking in the gutter, cars rushing by, only a few inches from mowing them down. This was live theatre, with an ever-changing cast of thousands.
London was frightening, exhilarating and totally foreign after spending the first 20 years of my life in the country. As I gingerly stepped off the bus in Shaftesbury Avenue and made my way onto Dean Street, I was entering an even stranger place. Soho is a tiny island. A village of little more than half a square mile. The streets are too narrow for fast-moving traffic and even today there is no public transport. Following the instructions I had been sent I made my way self-consciously towards Frith Street. As I struggled along with my heavy suitcase, I picked up snippets of conversations in a range of foreign languages. Soho had always attracted foreigners since the first houses had been built on Leicester and Windmill Fields. The French dominated, but Italians, Swiss and Greeks had also lived in the area for generations. White Russians who had escaped the revolution had also moved in. Now nationalities from all over the world had residents.
Somewhat bewildered, I made my way across Old Compton Street and into the road that was to become my home. There were exotic shops and restaurants offering every type of cuisine. Patisseries, kosher butchers, dressmakers and a shop selling records and sheet music. Lurking in doorways, girls whispered, “Hello, darling; looking for a good time?” Embarrassed and with head down I missed the building I was looking for and had to retrace my steps. Here people don’t

rush. Men pause, lighting cigarettes, eyeing the women, who paraded slowly, wearing very high heels and short skirts.
I knew I was to live above a grocery shop, and having worked at Jepson's in Stratton Market since I left school perhaps I was expecting to see something similar. De Monico's was more like a modern delicatessen. The windows were crammed with huge cheeses and the shelves of the small store were lined with bottles of tomatoes, olives, cooking oils and biscuits. A whole section was given over to fresh pastas and another to fruit. A bell attached to the door signalled my arrival. A tall, sullen man appeared from behind a bead curtain. I introduced myself. He ignored my outstretched hand. Reaching beneath the counter he handed me two keys on a ring
"Room six on the top floor. Use the side door – alright? I don't want you coming through the shop."
I nodded. "Can you tell me where I meet Mr Filkins in the morning?" He smiled for the first time.
"The Fat Man will be down in the basement at about eleven." He scowled. "Are you any good? I've never met an Englishman who can make real music. You have no soul."
"They tell me I can." He looked doubtful. He showed me out to the side door. A young man was furtively talking to a woman who looked old enough to be his mother. The back stairs were well worn. Linoleum capped with metal edges and banisters clammy to the touch. I lugged my suitcase up the unlit stairs, to the top floor. Peering through the gloom, I was passed by a small man dressed in a suit and a trilby pulled down over his face.
"Are you a punter?" The accent was Scottish. A small dark figure was standing at the doorway to number five. The light from her room threw out strange shadows and it was difficult to gauge her age. There was a vague smell of cooking, which had been eclipsed by a sweet, sickly perfume mixed with disinfectant.

"I'm looking for number six. I guess I'm your new neighbour." I could see her now. She was quite young. She had a face that looked as if it had never seen sunlight. She could have been quite pretty, but her eyes were too close together and her lips too thin. She had the look of someone who is permanently depressed.
"Och, you are the young musician, are you? Well, don'na practise all bleedy night, now, will you?"
She also ignored my outstretched hand. I thought how rude people in London were, but she did smile fleetingly as she closed the door. In that moment she suddenly looked very young. It was only later that it dawned on me that she had been wearing a gymslip.

* * * * * * * *

I had been playing at hunt balls since I was 14. They were grand affairs, drawing all the gentry and moneyed classes from across the county. Large house parties were organised and guests came up from London and further afield.
My playing had improved greatly and it was Mrs Champion who arranged for me to entertain the guests. Increasingly she looked on me as her protégé. Initially I provided background music, whilst the band rested and the guests ate. As the years progressed my spot was extended and I developed a cabaret routine. I had been to see Al Jolson in *The jazz singer* and all my spare money was spent on collecting the sheet music of the latest hits. I was allowed to listen to records on the Champions' wind-up gramophone. I copied the styles of those early stars, but the blues records that Mr William brought back from a business trip to America quite overwhelmed me. Every weekend I played at village dances. I experimented, upgrading and developing my act. My singing voice was pleasant but lacking any real style, but my

repertoire was growing and I was able to fill a half-hour spot without hesitation.
The venue for the hunt ball alternated between a variety of the grand local houses and the assembly rooms in Stratton Market. My mother and the rest of the staff were at full stretch as the time of the ball approached. The Champions always entertained one of the largest parties, extending up to some 20 couples. Many came up from London, including well-known writers and artists. The previous year the Champions had hosted the event for the first time. There had been a record attendance, with so many anxious to see the inside of the house. Some had looked forward to criticising the garish decor, but were silenced by the charm of what they saw. Not only was the house quite beautiful, but the food and entertainment lavish. William Champion glowed with pride at his wife's accomplishment.
The Champions' guests did, however, give an opportunity for tongues to wag. Augustus John had dressed as if he was about to do some gardening, defying etiquette and refusing to wear the conventional evening wear. He had been accompanied by one of his young models and had offended several ladies by his behaviour on the dance floor. Robert Graves, who had come over from his home in Majorca, sported a theatrical cloak and had drunk far too much. He had been sick into a basalt jardinière, pausing only to wipe his mouth with a silk handkerchief before continuing his dance with the daughter of the Lord Lieutenant of the county. Another guest was Harold Goldman and his wife. Goldman was a leading theatrical agent and impresario. Those connected with the theatre were thought of as being very suspect by the gentry, particularly if Jewish.
My performance had been very well received and I was touched that Mr Goldman took the trouble to seek me out later to congratulate me. At the time I had no idea who he was. The following day Mrs Champion requested that I should

perform again, up at the house after lunch. This time my audience consisted only of the Goldmans and Mrs Champion. It was more unnerving playing for just three people, rather than several hundred. I played numbers requested by the Goldmans. They covered a wide variety of styles and tunes. Some I sang, others I just played. They asked me for some of my favourites and I gave them Cole Porter's *What is this thing called love?* and *Weep no more, my baby*. It must have been an hour before I was dismissed. Harold Goldman shook my hand; "Keep at it, young man. I think one day you could make it."
"Harry, why don't you..," his wife began, but he silenced her with a wave of his hand.
"Keep at it, Mitch." No one had ever called me Mitch before. I had always been Bob, or even Robert when my mother was annoyed with me.
"Thank you, sir."
"Maybe I will see you next year?"
"I hope so, sir."
"And then maybe, just maybe..?"
"Sir?"
"Keep at it, young man; you have a talent."
"Thank you very much, sir."
Mrs Champion told me later what 'a big wheel' Harry Goldman was in the London entertainment world. I gave the matter very little thought, until I noticed Harry Goldman sitting at the Champions' table the following year at the assembly rooms. I had used the time well. There were new numbers and now I was able to hold an audience's attention. My time in countless village halls had not been wasted. As I finished my act, bowing, I noticed Lettice Champion leading the applause. Harry Goldman, a giant cigar in his mouth, was writing furiously in a notebook. Bowing again I saw my mother standing with a group of waitresses by the kitchen. She was crying.

I cycled home that night. Four miles, mostly uphill. Although it was a frosty night, I was sweating from my exertion. Kemp, the butler, was waiting for me and told me I was wanted in the library. Smoothing my dishevelled hair, I knocked on the door nervously. Mrs Champion was smiling and Mr William took my hand, pumping it vigorously. "Well done, Bob." I must have looked bemused, as Mr Goldman explained to me that he was prepared to offer me a month in London working under the legendary Fat Man Filkins. If, at the end of that time, he was impressed with me I would be offered a contract to work as a professional performer. I was speechless. My mother was called in and the proposal explained to her. She was worried about me giving up my job at Jepson's, but it was only a token protest. All of us in that room knew this was a break that would never come again. I was overcome with emotion. Casting convention aside, I took Mrs Champion in my arms. Without her help none of this would have been possible. For a moment I thought I had overstepped the mark. Connie looked horrified, but the men applauded. Mrs Champion lay her head on my chest. I could feel her tears on my shirt. We stood quite still, holding each other with the intensity of lovers.

* * * * * * * *

The Fat Man was huge. His sheer bulk, his watermelon smile, his laughter. Everything about the man was exaggerated. His personality alone would seem to fill a room. In the small basement in Frith Street his presence was overbearing. Well into his seventies, he had white cotton wool hair, which made his skin appear even darker. Suffering from poor sight from birth, he had finally gone totally blind a decade before. He wore dark glasses and carried a white stick, which seemed to act as his eyes. For a big man he moved sedately, somehow divining a path through the clogged Soho traffic.

As a young man, he had made a great name for himself in Harlem. He played the vaudeville theatres, nightclubs and bars. He accompanied Betty Smith on some of her early recordings. He influenced the likes of Fats Waller and James P Johnson. He was, perhaps, the first entertainer to use his right hand to improvise new themes, or chords of the melody, rather than just banging away to embellish the tune. Known as 'the daddy of the stride piano', he could romp, he could roll and his blues technique was copied and imitated by many who became more famous. His liking for booze and white girls were to prove his undoing. He described it to me as 'a pregnancy too far'. In any event he escaped to Europe, making Paris his home. As his eyes failed so his drink and drug intake accelerated, making it difficult for him to work. Harold Goldman signed him for a short season appearing in secondary night spots in the West End. The deal included a couple of hours' tuition a day for me.

On our first meeting his reputation alone was intimidating. He sat beside me. I felt inadequate and amateurish. I played two or three numbers before he made any comment.

"That was shit, man." I was crushed, knowing he was right. He dissolved into a crumpled, heaving laughing mass. Seeing I was quite mortified, he squeezed my arm.

"Relax, Mitch. Just slow things down, man. Right now, try again."

I did, again and again. He chortled as I played; sometimes he joined me in the lyrics. He talked, encouraged and laughed non-stop. I was sure I would be on the next train home. After what seemed hours, he took my hands in his. It would have looked strange to anyone entering that dingy basement. His fingers probed mine. He paid particular attention to the backs of my hands. We didn't speak. I felt as if he was trying to transmit some of his talent. Gently he placed my hands back on the keyboard. Then he pulled the piano stool out slightly.

My arms were more extended. I felt uncomfortable, my feet hardly reaching the pedals.
"Right, Mitch; nice and slow, real relaxed. Give me *Night and day*." He laughed all the way through the number, his belly bouncing. "Yeah, man, that's better. That's my boy, Mitch. I like it."
Turning, I saw Antonio the shopkeeper standing by the door. "Hey, the English boy can make music."
"He's shit," the Fat Man roared, "but he'll do. I'll have him playing like a black man soon."
"And singing like an Italian?" Antonio queried.
"No, man; that Mr Goldman wants him to have the voice of an English toff."

* * * * * * * *

Harry Goldman was right. My singing voice retained the flat Midland vowels. I was dispatched twice a week to Kentish Town, to get elocution lessons from a 'resting' actress. Edwina Binder's flat was dominated by huge Victorian furniture, potted plants and cats. I was quick to pick up an 'upper crust' accent. I had been surrounded by well-spoken people all my life. I had been too embarrassed to speak 'posh' at home, for fear of being ragged by my friends. Edwina was impressed with the speed of my conversion, so she spent much of her time teaching me how to attract and hold an audience. Everything, every movement, had to be at what she called 'seven eights'. Movements and speech were all to be conducted at a speed that felt slower than normal. Sitting down at the piano, bowing to the audience, the placing of the hands on the piano – nothing to be rushed. It was similar advice to that given by the Fat Man. I even started to get out of bed slowly. Shaving was a study in a series of relaxed strokes, with my cut-throat razor. By the second week I was really beginning to enjoy myself. The Fat Man was now

getting me to play in total darkness. He insisted that I play not only like a black man, but a blind one at that.
I had been in London about three weeks when I was called to Harry Goldman's office in Denman Street. He told me the reports from the Fat Man and Edwina had been favourable. He had also eavesdropped on one of my sessions and had been impressed. Then, in time-honoured tradition, he told me he was going to make me a star. Surrounded by billboards and glamorous photographs of some of the stars he handled, I think I believed him. He informed me he was intending sending me on a summer tour of the south coast. Providing this went well, he intended launching me in London in the autumn. He then produced a contract for me to sign and called his secretary in to be a witness. There is a feeling amongst Londoners that anyone from the country is not too bright. My experience is that country folk tend to be very cautious and are not easily led. I listened to the risks he was taking on my behalf. The costs were considerable. Rent, hotels, new clothes, transport; the list was endless. Whilst not wanting to appear ungrateful, I couldn't imagine Mr William signing a contract without taking advice. I didn't know if 25% was standard for a manager to take from a performer, but it seemed a lot to me. I told Mr Goldman I needed some advice and would come back to him. He started to protest, but then broke into a broad smile. "You do that, son. You know I like you. I have a feeling you are going to be really big. I feel it right here," and he pressed at his fat belly, enclosed in an expensive double-breasted waistcoat. I hoped he was right.
The general perception is that London can be a very lonely place. Soho wasn't. Everyone was friendly, once you were part of the scene. Antonio arranged for me to meet an Italian lawyer. "He's a powerful man. You understand? Nobody messes with him."
The lawyer, Enrico Bertoni, was tall, dark and elegant. He had what my mother would have called surgeon's hands.

Long, splayed fingers, which caressed the files piled high on his desk. He also had eyes like a caged animal, which remained wary whilst his features impersonated a smile. His face had no laughter lines, but his brow was furrowed. He negotiated a deal, where I paid Harry Goldman 15% for the first year and 10% for the next four. He was also to retain 1% for himself. Country boy I might be, but I knew that Mr Bertoni was not someone to argue with. "I will watch over you," he said, pressing my flesh. I believed him. Walking out of his office, through the typing pool, I was conscious of a number of tough-looking individuals sitting round a table by the entrance. The receptionist informed me they were legal assistants. Over the next couple of years I often saw these assistants collecting rents from the street girls.

I was now given a small weekly allowance, which enabled me to leave my rather claustrophobic room more often. I couldn't help being conscious of some of the activity from number five. Indistinct conversations, the occasional arguments, and strange thumpings. I had seen my neighbour just three or four times since I moved in. She would parade the length of the street, hair in plaits, sporting a gymslip, white shirt, ankle socks and high heels. She always returned with a customer, and others presumably took their turn. She seldom had to parade for a second time. There were two more girls on the first floor, who were friendlier when I passed them on the stairs. They made alarming suggestions to me, but only at a price. My experience with the opposite sex on my arrival in London had been confined to fevered kissing and groping with some of the local girls after dances. Most girls (at least, the ones I met) didn't, and I was still extremely unworldly.

I had started going for the odd drink at the Dog and Duck after my prolonged practice sessions. This was one of the oldest pubs in Soho, situated on the corner of Frith Street and Bateman Street. I ordered a pint in the public bar; I could

hear a load of banter and laughter coming from the saloon. I saw a familiar face duck under the rack of hanging glasses.
"Ignoring us, are you, wee music man? Come on in, don't be shy." There were about half a dozen girls sitting round a table littered with glasses.
"This is my neighbour, girls. The gorgeous 'Mitch'." How did she know my name? She looked quite different. Her hair was hanging loose down to her shoulders, and she wore a short dress. I felt my colour rise in embarrassment.
"He's a bit of alright."
"Ain't he cute?"
"How about a quickie, luvvy? Good discount for a friend of Eve's."
So, Eve was her name. They looked me over, like a farmer viewing a beast at market. I offered to buy them a drink, but they bought me one instead.
"I bet you don't have to pay for it, do you, love?" The woman who was probably the oldest of the group raised her glass to me.
"Hey, cut that out," the barman snapped. "This is a respectable pub."
They were all tipsy and they laughed almost too heartily, I felt. They were really rather sad. They met for an hour each lunchtime. This was their 'off duty' time and they would turn on anyone who tried to proposition them. Over the next few weeks I joined them regularly. They could be boisterous, funny, vulgar, and sad when reviewing with great honesty where their lives had gone wrong. They were caught in a trap of high rents, demanding pimps and a constant threat of violence. They all insisted that this was just a lousy phase in their life. They all dreamt of the day when they would have enough money to walk away. To buy that dress shop, or – better still – marry a kind, rich punter and live happily ever after in the suburbs. Soho was hard work, but Edgware or Esher were heaven.

A few of the girls came to the basement to hear me practise before they went on duty. They were my earliest fans and touchingly protective of me. The Fat Man told them I was going to be a star and they believed him. These normally hard-faced women vied for my friendship. They presumably didn't find me threatening. I went shopping in Berwick Street with Bea and Alice. I made odd visits to the pictures with Eve and Carol. They all loved romantic movies, and yet outside the cinema they showed a resentment towards men, coloured – no doubt – by the acts they had to perform.

Prostitutes were generally treated with respect and as equals by most of the residents in Soho. The Jewish community, centred around Berwick Street, could sometimes be rather offhand, whilst the Italians and Greeks, who watched their daughters like hawks, existed happily enough alongside the street girls. My new friends were all British and came about halfway up the whores' hierarchy. The really high-class girls were found in Mayfair, around Curzon Street. In Soho the French girls. or 'fifies', were at the top of the tree, whilst the half-crown girls on Lisle Street were considered the dregs.

Bea was the quietest of the girls. A tall, attractive redhead in her early thirties. Although I spent many hours in her company she never talked about her background, other than to say she had come to London from Bristol a couple of years before. She was ragged by the other girls because a couple of times a year she went back to the West Country, demurely dressed, presumably to see her family. She had a reputation for being a tough cookie, good in a scrap and ruthless with the punters. I liked her company. To me she seemed rather gentle, helped, no doubt, by her soft Bristol accent. She loved music and was the most regular visitor to hear me practise. She would sit through whole sessions as the Fat Man put me through my paces. During the sessions her hard-faced mask would drop. Her feet would tap in time to the music and her

expression showed she was off in some private place created in her mind.
Eve had been due to join us for the early performance of a film starring Ramon Navarro at the Empire, Leicester Square. At the last moment she decided to go to the pub instead. The film was a huge disappointment. When we appeared from the upper circle we were greeted by pouring rain. It showed no sign of clearing so we made a run for it. Heads down, we charged across the square and into Soho. Most people were sheltering in doorways, but we were soaked already so we continued. By the time we crossed Shaftesbury Avenue Bea was lagging behind. Taking her hand I pulled her along, laughing, panting and swearing in quick succession. As we reached the entrance to her flat in Bateman Street her hair was matted and flattened. Her face was quite red from exertion. "Fancy a cuppa?" she asked, and I followed her into the darkened stair well. The flat was warm and tidy. She went into the bathroom to change and I was left to make the tea on a small gas ring in the tiny living room. Through the door I could make out a double bed and an ornate dressing table that took up almost all the floor space. The sitting room had pottery souvenirs covering every available surface. Ashtrays from Brighton and vases from Blackpool. Many of the knick-knacks came from around the world: New York, Cannes, St Moritz. I assumed some of her regulars brought these for her, as I was sure that Bea had never been abroad. Marooned amidst this sea of pottery were two photographs. One of a young boy, smiling nervously at the camera minus his front teeth. The other was of the young Bea caught in the backyard of a terraced house. Head tilted to one side she smiles at the camera. Taken in her teens, she is pretty, an open, cheeky expression on her face. A young woman confident of her place in the world and the life to come.
It was my fault that things happened the way they did. With the bedroom door still ajar, I caught a glimpse of her drying

herself. Sitting at the dressing table she tossed her wet towel onto the bed. With her eyes shut she brushed her hair back off her face with long, slow strokes. For an incongruous moment it reminded me of my mother. The rhythm was therapeutic. Silently I moved into the room. I couldn't help myself. I had never seen a woman naked before. Sensing me, she stared at my reflection in the mirror for what seemed an age. Turning, she said, "Oh, alright then." There was a sense of resignation in her voice.

I was hopeless. I rushed, I was clumsy. I felt terrible, for as I finished she started to cry. Her body was convulsed and her freshly applied make-up smudged. I knew I had ruined one of the few innocent relationships in her life. I stroked her wet hair and tried to comfort her. "I'm so sorry," I kept repeating.

"It's only me." A voice called from the living room. I froze. "Who left this kettle boiling?"

It was Bea's maid. All the girls employed one to cut down the risk of violence.

"I'm alright, Elsie." I started to get out of the bed, but Bea pulled me back. She handed me a handkerchief and I wiped away her smudged mascara. She looked much older without make-up.

"Don't tell any of the other girls about this, will you?"

"No, I promise."

"If you do I'll get you sorted. Understand?" I nodded. "Good; let's see if you can do any better this time, shall we?"

I didn't protest. "Here; give me your hand and I'll show you which buttons to press." She laughed, but her expression was hard, contemptuous. She guided, orchestrated me, but her manner was aggressive. "Slowly," she barked; "it's not a bleeding race." I remembered the Fat Man's and Edwina's advice. Her anger gradually dissolved. "That's it. That's better. There, there." Her voice was a whisper now.

"You alright, Bea?" Elsie enquired.

“Sod off,” Bea shouted, and I joined her, but my cries were on being introduced to an entirely new world. As we lay apart on the bed, I confessed to her that it had been my first time.
“Well, what a surprise,” she said, giving a coarse laugh. I felt mortified.
“Cheer up,” she said. “They say you never forget the first time. So, when you’re rich and famous, remember me, you little bugger, won’t you?”
“I will,” I said; and I have.

CHAPTER 9

It's *not* a foggy day in London town! Warm autumn sunlight filters through my window. I decide against an afternoon nap. Well wrapped up, I venture out of the hotel into Leicester Square. The tramps have gone off in search of more Export lagers.

On the bench opposite mine a young man reads and rereads a handwritten airmail letter, as if it is about to reveal the meaning of life. Is it a love letter? Or one that tells him he's history? He mouths the words silently, as if he has just learnt to read. A young woman sits beside me and she unwraps a sandwich from a cellophane container. Having taken one bite she throws the crusts on the ground, for the tame birds that peck and fight for the scraps. Now she parts the remains of the sandwich and looks suspiciously at the contents. Pulling a face, she deposits the rejected sandwich into the metal bin beside me, before rushing off. Closing my eyes, the noise of perpetual footsteps and the vague hum of distant traffic are strangely comforting.

* * * * * * * *

The morning after my adventure at the boating lake my very worst fears were confirmed. We were visited by our local constable, accompanied by a plain-clothes detective. My mother looked on, quite horrified, whilst they established that I had been at the boathouse. Had I permission? I was frightened. I knew I shouldn't have broken in but I had no idea that it would lead to so much trouble. Constable Margeston told us that Lady Dorothy was furious and that we were to present ourselves at the hall at midday. I was convinced that I would be sent away to a Borstal, at the very least. Then it became clear that the police were not interested in my trespassing. Earlier in the morning there had been a well-organised robbery at the hall. The thieves had been very selective, taking only items of solid silver and Lady Dorothy's most valuable jewellery. They questioned me for ages. Had I seen anyone lurking in the woods? Had I spoken to any strangers? Later I found out Kitty had also been subjected to a similar cross-examination. For days the papers were full of the story of what had been a highly professional job. The *Daily Mail* suggested the gang must have had some inside help, as they had gained entry through an open door onto the terrace. They also knew exactly where to find the most valuable but easily transportable items. Eventually the policemen seemed to accept that I had nothing of value to tell them.

Whilst the interrogation by the police was worrying, the interview with Lady Gibbs was terrifying. We were kept waiting in a small room in the servants' quarters for what seemed an age. Then the haughty butler led us down darkened corridors to Sir Percy's study. It was a dark, north-facing room, made more sombre by the ancient wood panelling.

"The Mitchell boy and his mother, madam." I wished my mother hadn't curtsied, but she was almost more worried than I was. She looked very pale as she stared straight ahead at the vast figure of Lady Dorothy, squeezed behind her husband's desk. For a moment she ignored us, pretending to read from a leather-bound book in front of her. Then she stood and, without speaking, circled us, the room quite silent but for the rustle of her dress. Suddenly she started firing questions at me. Who had given me permission to go to the lake? Why were Kitty and I always plaguing her son? Did we not realise he was ill? I tried to stumble out replies, but she silenced me with an imperious wave of the hand.

My mother tried to calm her by suggesting how upset Lady Dorothy must be by the robbery.

“Upset, woman, by losing a few trinkets? Rubbish! I tell you what has upset me: your wretched son.”
“But, madam, I’m sure he meant no harm. He only went for a swim.”
“Has he not told you?” My mother looked confused.
“What, madam? Please don’t upset yourself. What?”
Lady Dorothy’s bosom was vast and now it was heaving alarmingly. Tears of anger and frustration ran down her cheeks.
“He broke into the boathouse – that’s what. No one, not a soul, has been in there for eight years. Nothing was to be touched. It was a shrine to daddy, who died there. It has been desecrated.”
“I’m so sorry; I’m sure the boy didn’t know.”
“Not content with that,” Lady Dorothy continued, “he then proceeded to dance naked. I know; I saw him, and so did my son. He was most distressed.”
“I wasn’t dancing; someone took my clothes. I just ran back to the boathouse after swimming. I didn’t mean any harm.” I started crying.
She must have rung a bell because the butler appeared and we were dismissed. I was told I was a wicked boy, abusing hospitality. If I went on like this I would end up a criminal. I was no longer to be allowed into the grounds. Her strangest criticism, though, suggested that in some way I had attempted to lead Evelyn astray.
“Flaunting yourself like that.”
I had no idea what she was talking about. Neither did I understand my mother’s cross-questioning of me on our way home. It was many years before the penny dropped.
It was only a few days after the robbery that we learned that the Prince of Wales was coming up from London to stay at the hall. The Stratton Hunt was well regarded and the Prince was due to stay until Saturday, to enable him to get two full days’ hunting in. Miss Ormerod was beside herself and Mr William

had given his staff an hour off to welcome the prince when he arrived at Stratton Market station. Mr Curtis brought in teams of cleaners. Platforms were scrubbed and swept. The whole station was repainted and flowers were displayed in window boxes, wilting within hours due to the cold. We were all issued with small Union Jacks on sticks, to wave. We stood outside in the rain as the Rolls-Royce Sir Percy had hired for the occasion swept by.

Thursday's hunting was deemed a great success and Friday was to be given over to civic visits. No one knew why a visit to the local cottage hospital had been cancelled, but the chairman of governors arrived to tell a dumbstruck Miss Ormerod that the prince was to visit our school instead. Her face came out in blotches at the thought. Hurriedly a programme of inspection was planned, to be rounded off by me accompanying the school in a rousing version of the national anthem.

We were all sent home at lunchtime to change into our best clothes. Our nails were inspected and our hair picked over for 'nits'. The official party was 20 minutes late, by which time Miss Ormerod was shaking in anticipation. Strangely, I was not nervous. Playing the piano was about the only thing I did well. The prince was almost submerged by the group of dignitaries surrounding him. They pressed into our small schoolroom, for the most part looking ill at ease and out of place. He was shorter than I had expected. He had a friendly face, though, breaking into a roguish grin when Miss Ormerod curtsied so deeply that for a moment it appeared she might topple over. His manner was very natural and he appeared genuinely interested as he inspected the exercise books that Miss Ormerod had decreed were fit for royal scrutiny. I was sitting at the piano, waiting for the signal from my teacher. He spotted me and asked, "Are you going to give us a tune?"

Miss Ormerod coloured. "Your Majesty, Robert will play the national anthem, so that all the school can join in."

"What else can you play?"
"Chopin, Mozart?" The teacher suggested.
"Anything more up to date?"
"Yes, sir."
"Your Highness," Miss Ormerod whispered, "how about *Alexander's ragtime band*?"
Straightaway I broke into the tune, while the prince conducted the school as all the pupils joined in. The guests and Miss Ormerod looked somewhat embarrassed and only applauded politely as we came to a raucous finale. He shook my hand and congratulated me. Neither of us could have guessed that I would be playing for him again many times over the years, in settings very different from our village schoolroom.

* * * * * * * * *

Strangely, the first clip I am shown at the studio in Newman Street also features the Prince of Wales. I am picked out fleetingly, looking incredibly young, before the camera pans to the prince and his party. I imagine the film must date to about 1935 and I think the venue was Pops, a fashionable nightclub in Soho Square. I am playing *I only have eyes for you*. The soundtrack is poor and I am embarrassed by how studied my upper-class delivery is. It was years later that I reminded the prince of our first meeting. He had a throwaway sense of humour. "I think you were better as a kid, Mitch, actually." All his acolytes fell about laughing, and, of course, I joined in. He was a keen amateur drummer in those days, often joining the resident band when he had drunk enough to give himself the confidence.
Another clip captures Edwina Mountbatten singing *Anything goes* with me. She sits on top of the piano, legs dangling. She was a wild, vivacious woman, about whom much has been written. I could add to that, but I was much too fond of her to do so. We are filmed just before the outbreak of war. I was at

the height of my career, earning up to £700 per week. Much of my money was spent on clothes. I had over 20 tailed suits for performing alone.

It is strange viewing myself all those years ago. I feel very detached. It is like watching a stranger. They have located a very early film of me cutting my first recording. I am surrounded by a bank of massive microphones and a jumbled sea of wires. I am giving a passable performance of *You're the cream in my coffee.*

The researchers have done well. Next I am shown playing at a private party. I didn't exactly sing for my supper at these gatherings. There tended to be other rewards bestowed by my hostess. I was a trophy to be shown off. Never really accepted in the highest of circles, but I could pass muster at a push, particularly when I was young and attractive. Stephanie Aston wanted to know where the house was. It was certainly very grand. High, vaulted ceilings with elaborate chandeliers hanging on heavy chains and a glimpse of an early Munnings in the background. It was only when Angela Dudley moved into shot to give me a peck on the cheek that I remembered. Angela was the youngest daughter of a leading shipping magnate. The house was a substantial Georgian manor house, just outside Harpenden. The kiss Angela gives me on camera looks platonic enough, but generally Lady Angela didn't rate innocent friendships.

I remember accompanying her on several occasions whilst she sang in her little schoolgirl voice.

Love for sale
Who will buy?
Who would like to sample my supply?
Who's prepared to pay the price
For a trip to paradise?

Like most of her society contemporaries, Angela had been brought up to observe a strict social code. Servants should be treated correctly. You should show an interest in them, even be fond of them, but never get involved with them romantically. Angela went against all this advice. She was vile to those in her employ. She was spoilt, unreasonable and paid the staff wretched wages. She did, however, have a tendency to bed the most attractive of them, of both sexes. Once her use for them had been spent, they were dismissed on the flimsiest pretext. I was rather alarmed that she saw through the veneer of my accent and new-found fame. She urged me to verbally abuse her. She wanted to be given rough treatment. I didn't like the games she played. She was outrageous and oblivious to what others thought of her, including her husband. Amazingly, their marriage survived numerous, highly publicised scandals. In later years the couple were inseparable, devoting most of their time to animal charities.

Stephanie Aston appears to be shocked by my revelations. It was a time when the rich and famous indulged in bizarre behaviour. Was this a generation still trying to forget the horror of war, or the last ritual dance of the sons and daughters of the aristocracy?

I am amazed at how much they have of me on film. We agree on the best couple of clips. Then, up on the screen, is film of my marriage. This is another side of my life I have conveniently pushed to the very back of my mind. What a motley group, grinning and swaying outside St Marleybone registry office on a sunny winter's morning in 1940.

"Tell me about your marriage," Stephanie prompts. The footage is short. I ask her to run it through again. She can sense I am unsettled by these memories. She freezes the frame. Some of the group I can't even remember. I do recollect most of us were drunk. The registrar had threatened to cancel the ceremony if we didn't stop giggling. Our best

man, Eric Madden, stares unseeing at the camera. Luckily, he was sick out of shot. No wonder my mother looks so old and unwell. The poor darling was dead within three months. How insensitive I was, how selfish. I am full of my own self-importance. My Savile Row suit might as well have come from the '50 bob' tailors. I have put on weight and the expensive cloth is under pressure to contain my burgeoning belly. Dolores is on my arm. Did I feel I was betraying Kitty at that time? Probably not. I sought refuge in the bottle and dubious friends.
"Tell me about Dolores Allingham." Stephanie asks. I am being filmed. The lights have been turned up. I haven't noticed the camera. What can I say about Dolores? This is a part of my life I don't want put under scrutiny. Perhaps a sanitised version. Dolores was an American actress I had known since my early days in London She tended to get supporting or cameo roles in West End shows. She was 12 years older than me but still good-looking. Her career was in something of a crisis. The transition from romantic to character roles is particularly difficult for actresses. It was never more than a marriage of convenience. I was on the rebound and she was looking for financial stability. I thought she was kind and intelligent and she thought I was rich. We bought a house in Highgate. Her career started to take off again. We rarely saw each other. She was always on tour. "We remained good friends after the divorce," I conclude lamely.
"That's not what she said. If you're not able to explain why you married, why did you divorce?" I was beginning to feel very uncomfortable.
"I think you know why."
"Tell us, please."
Facing the camera, I falteringly tell my unseen audience that I did indeed marry as the result of a true romance, which ended in tragedy. I'm glad Stephanie doesn't press me on this point.

I also knew my mother was dying and Dolores seemed to offer the comfort and understanding I was seeking. Our professional engagements kept us apart and, in truth, we lived what today are described as separate lives. When we were together we enjoyed each other's company. I was at the top of my career, earning a massive £40,000 a year. Then the war came.
"And you dodged call-up, didn't you?"
This is what the programme has been leading up to. I am to be pilloried. My epitaph: not Mitch the cabaret star, but Mitch the coward.
I continued to explain that Dolores, although American, was the ultimate anglophile. A true British patriot. I was approaching 30 and she was convinced that I should join up as soon as possible. It is difficult to remember my frame of mind at the time. I know I had just secured a new record contract with HMV and Harry Goldman had booked me for the best part of the following year. He suggested I visit a Dr Richardson, in Harley Street. For a sizeable fee, he diagnosed that I was suffering from epilepsy. I was excused war service and was able to continue my career. I thought the war would be over in months, that I was just being pragmatic and certainly not cowardly. Dolores was disgusted. She threw tantrums and told anyone who was prepared to listen that I was a disgrace to my country. Her generous divorce settlement required that she no longer spread rumours about me. London society is almost like a small village, and considerable damage to my reputation was done.
Throughout the rest of the war and into the early fifties my career went into a gentle decline. My recording contract was not renewed in 1949 and I was beginning to play venues that previously I would not have considered. I wasn't shunned by society, but neither was I welcomed. My looks had coarsened. I had a weight problem. I was looked on as old-

fashioned. New young stars were arriving. New sounds; the world was changing.
By 1952 I was reduced to summer seaside shows, theatrical digs and the occasional conquest of women that, ten years earlier, I wouldn't even have paused to give my autograph to.
My professional death knell came with the arrest of Dr Richardson, for possessing and distributing cocaine. Skipping bail, he fled to Marbella, from where he sold his story to the *News of the World.* He had supplied drugs to film stars, politicians and even a senior member of the Church of England. The second instalment in the paper dealt with sex parties and orgies he had arranged for the rich and famous. The effects were seismic; call-girls and politicians dominated the daily news. By the third instalment the spiciest details had already been revealed, but this short article was finally to kill off my career. He divulged the names of the well-connected people who had been excused war service by his false diagnoses. They included captains of industry, a politician, a champion boxer – and me. I was the most famous. I had no defence. I went to visit friends in South Africa.
Returning six months later, I found the furore had died down. I did get some bookings, but now I could only command £40 a week. It was the time of the Korean War, and I tried to make amends by undertaking long and often dangerous tours entertaining the troops. At home I constantly performed for charity. My stock in the public's eye began to rise, but then rock and roll arrived. I was finished. It was time to retire gracefully. I was drinking too much and I decided to seek a warmer climate.
Stephanie raises her hand and the camera stops. "Mitch, that was superb. I hope you didn't mind my line of questioning."
I am shaking. "None of it matters anymore." Why am I losing my self-control? She allows me to regain my composure.
"Let's have a wash and brush-up, before we meet Sally."

I nod. Sally. Good God, her partner is a woman. Why should that shock me? The young can't invent anything that hasn't been done before.

* * * * * * * * *

Sally is a lawyer. A beautiful, amusing, fun-to-be-with lawyer. The girls are completely at ease with each other. They tease, but show no overt feelings in public. They have brought me to a Spanish restaurant, sensing I might be a little homesick. They are kind. The food is excellent and I am enjoying myself. I show off my fluent Spanish.
Over coffee we discuss plans for tomorrow. We seem to have shot enough film for a five-hour programme, but it will all be condensed into a 50-minute slot. I tell Stephanie the programme is obviously not going to be as bland as I had supposed.
"Will you have any more surprises for me?"
She smiles. "I think I might." And she did.

CHAPTER 10

I can't sleep. In my restlessness, the sheets have become rumpled and form ridges that push against my sore kidneys. I drank too much last night, but that is not the reason. I am terrified of falling asleep. Eventually I do drift off, waking with a start, my heart thumping. It is as if I think this slumber will be my last. Why do I worry? I shouldn't be afraid of death; I have had plenty of time to contemplate it.

I have no real beliefs. Perhaps it is the clergy I have encountered, rather than Christianity, that has left me feeling cheated. Being a serious-minded youngster, Kitty had always been fascinated by religion. Although brought up in the Church of England, she continued to be influenced by her mother. She was adamant that each of us possesses a single soul, which goes through a series of incarnations. After bodily death the soul lives on, taking with it a series of impressions. These are reborn when the soul reincarnates and help to decide the type of person we are to be in the next life.

I don't know if I really believe that, either. Nonetheless, I feel I am being propelled along a road that will eventually reveal the truth about what really happened to Kitty.

* * * * * * * *

Each year one or two children from our school won scholarships to Stratton Market Grammar School. This was always a source of pride for Miss Ormerod and a reward for her undoubted teaching ability. It was no surprise that Kitty had passed the entrance exam, but to gain entry to the 'A' stream was unprecedented. On her last day at the village school, Kitty received the year's prize from the chairman of the governors. The village hall was packed for the prize-giving. There were awards for each age group and also for sporting achievements. Miss Ormerod was perhaps too gushing in her praise of Kitty and the wide choice of educational opportunities that awaited her. Most of the pupils at the school were destined to be qualified only to undertake menial jobs, and the downturned mouths of their parents indicated resentment. Kitty looked embarrassed as she climbed the steps onto the stage to collect her prize. Although her parents smiled proudly it was noticeable that the applause from the audience was muted. Whilst I was impressed by Kitty's achievements, I was sad as I realised that I would be seeing far less of her in the future.

It was at about this time that my musical education received a further boost and gave Miss Ormerod another pupil to boast about. Miss Cecily Procter was a dancing teacher. Not of ballet, but of ballroom dancing. As well as holding evening classes in Stratton Market, her Saturdays were devoted to visiting local public schools. Ballroom dancing was considered to be a necessity for all the well-to-do young. Miss Procter had lost her regular accompanist and had heard of my developing prowess. Each Saturday morning we would board a train for Oundle, Uppingham or Wellingborough. Miss Procter would sit in first-class, whilst I was stationed in the sparser surroundings of the third-class compartment. We were normally met at the station by a pony and trap. Again, I was astounded by the disparity between what the children of the rich enjoyed compared with their working-class contemporaries. The schools were housed in imposing old buildings, with quadrangles, gymnasiums, tuck shops, plus endless classrooms and studies. Playing fields stretched into the distance. Perhaps a dozen games of cricket or rugby, all being undertaken at the same time. The masters I found frightening. Clothed in flowing black gowns and mortarboards, they seemed intent on instilling a discipline into their pupils that made Miss Ormerod seem positively benign.

The dancing lessons tended to be held in the main assembly hall. No girls ever attended. To either their intense embarrassment or amusement, the boys were taught to waltz, quickstep and foxtrot. The younger or slighter boys had to act as girls. I never quite understood how they learnt the male steps. Presumably, as they grew older or increased in stature, they were partnered by a boy from a lower year. Miss Procter moved among the stumbling couples, replacing an arm here and occasionally relieving a boy, so she could demonstrate with his partner how the steps were to be undertaken. At least two masters stood on the sidelines, looking hawkishly for any unseemly behaviour. There tended to be much suppressed giggling as the boys held each other tight, looking quite incongruous. I had heard dark mutterings from my village friends about what went on at public schools, and my visits tended to endorse their feelings. As I played my Strauss waltzes it was impossible not to be aware of an overbearing sense of repressed sexual feeling, with all these young men locked away together for weeks on end.

Like their masters, most of the boys ignored me. They stared at me in that way that those with power and influence reserve for the less fortunate, learnt, no doubt, from their fathers. Some were openly condescending, whilst just a few were approachable and friendly. I was conscious of how parochial I looked in my unfashionable hand-me-down clothes.

As I played and they danced, tripping over each other's feet, I was drawn to the endless honours boards that disappeared into the darkness of the vaulted ceilings. Names of students from the previous century who had gained entry to Oxford or Cambridge, scholars, boxing champions, cricket captains. The schools pointed students to a life of success and privilege. A life that most of us were excluded from. Some of these young men were probably brilliant, but the majority certainly not, and yet they all seemed to have one characteristic that I envied. They all appeared to carry themselves with a certain confidence. For months I watched them, memorising their speech and mannerisms. One day I would join them. I didn't

know how, but it sparked a desire to better myself that had never been apparent previously.
Miss Ormerod was so embarrassing. Each Monday I had to regale the school with details of my most recent visit. She obtained photographs of each establishment and uncovered details of their most famous old boys. To her, these men were the epitome of the establishment and all that it represented. We reserved our admiration for the film stars that we were now able to see at the new picture house in Stratton Market. The silver screen was our escape route from what was still largely a dull, hard and uncomfortable existence.
I saw less of Kitty now that she had started at her new school. Until then we had been together almost every day, since she arrived in the village. Suddenly I saw a new Kitty. More detached and serious, less fun, not so cheeky. She had new friends. I sensed she found me boring, irritating even. Physically she had changed, too. Although still short she carried herself with a natural poise. She was wearing her hair longer and it gleamed with health, tied back from her face with a blue ribbon. She was quite the young lady. I was still a boy.
Change was everywhere. Increased motor transport had led to our blacksmith closing down to seek employment at Champion's. The wheelwright business that had been in the village since the 18th century went bankrupt. We were no longer a self-contained unit. The modern world encroached from all sides. Ten council houses were built for agricultural workers. Electricity came to Champion House, followed shortly by the telephone. My mother remained wary of the instrument for years, leaping back in fright as the bell signalled an incoming call. "It doesn't seem natural," she would say; "it's just not right."
I missed Kitty's companionship so much. Life didn't seem right to me, either.

****

The local point-to-point races and the hunt ball were held on the same day. In the evening I earned a guinea for my cabaret act, but I also loved the excitement of the races. They were held on land two miles east of the village owned by the Gibbs family. The course was maintained all year by the tenant farmer and was one of the finest in the country. The track lay in a valley, surrounded on all sides by gentle banks, rising to create a natural stadium. Large crowds came each year. Cars and coaches vied at the entrance with horseboxes and pony traps. Others walked for miles on foot. It was one of the few occasions that people from all spheres of society mingled together, in shared enjoyment. Even then there was segregation. The members' enclosure was packed with butlers and staff laying out the most lavish picnics. Tables were covered with fine linen and food was eaten from china plates. Hams and sides of beef were carved, champagne corks popped. Others sat by their cars enjoying more modest fare from wicker hampers. The less well off brought sandwiches or congregated in the giant beer tent.

Away from the paddock colourful gypsy caravans parked, and, outside, dark women with skins of leather read palms or stared into glittering glass balls. Bookies shouted out the odds. There was noise everywhere, accents from across the social divide. Hounds barking as they were paraded by the pink-coated huntsmen. There were well-cut tweed suits, plus fours, men in collarless shirts and braces with sleeves rolled up, and even an old-timer in a traditional shepherd's smock. Women dressed in colourful floral frocks and wide hats. Pretty housemaids, corpulent butlers and red-faced farmers. The whole world was here.

It was the year after Kitty had started at her new school that the two great families of the village pitted themselves against each other for the first time. The members' race was open

only to those who hunted regularly with the Stratton. Normally it was of a lower standard than the open events, which attracted entries from miles around. These tended to be contested by expert riders on horses in regular training.
Fred Champion had won the event the previous two years, in spite of being a relatively poor rider. His mother had an excellent eye for a horse, buying regularly over in Ireland. The opposition tended to be poor and, provided he could stay on, victory was assured. This year was different. Whilst several tenant farmers had entered as usual, to provide token opposition, two members who came up from London to hunt had entered. Their mounts were of a different class. Gordon Dexter, a banker, was riding a huge, well-bred chestnut called Maximus. Nigel Crowther was the son of the chairman of Britain's leading brewers, a young man who devoted his life to hunting and point-to-point events. His horse, Hat Box, a sleek black filly, was out of a former classic winner and had been made favourite by the bookies. The real surprise was the entry of Evelyn Gibbs, riding his favourite mount, Top Score. Although he was a natural sportsman and a fine rider it was a testing course, and to attempt it with only one arm was considered madness.
I led Fred Champion's horse around the paddock, whilst the groom kept an eye on me. He had buffed the colt up so that its coat shone and had also neatly plaited its mane. He had duly won the best-turned-out award, and so I was hanging onto the reins whilst the groom waited to collect his prize. The horse was beginning to get excited and was sweating up. As the riders came into the paddock I was convinced that only Crowther's horse was going to be a match for Mr Fred's mount. Evelyn, looking very pale and gaunt, walked right past me without any sign of recognition. I gave Fred Champion a leg-up and the runners made their way through the crowds towards the start. The race was run over two and a half laps of the course. There were six large fences to be

negotiated on each lap, plus a water jump. Normally the race was undertaken at a pedestrian pace, but this year a young farmer, Ned Harrison, decided to try and steal the event. He set off at a great gallop, throwing his mount at the fences and opening up a big gap by the time they approached the finishing straight for the first time. I noticed that the London banker sat right back in the saddle, tugging savagely at his horse's mouth. I had heard him boasting earlier that he never fell off. Over each obstacle he landed pitching forward, but somehow managing to stay aboard. Two horses fell at the fifth fence and Ned's lead had increased to some 12 lengths as he flew the water jump, in front of the cheering crowds.
Fred Champion was now setting off in serious pursuit, and he was gaining until he hit the fence on the turn to the back straight, parting the birch. Nigel Crowther's mount was moving effortlessly in third place, alongside Evelyn, whose horse was already off the bit. By the time the six remaining horses reached the back straight for the last time Ned Harrison's horse had run its race. Hunched and ungainly, Fred Champion moved up alongside. The huge chestnut, Maximus, was now putting in a serious effort. Gordon Dexter sat back in the saddle, legs flapping and already resorting to the whip. Nigel Crowther seemed unconcerned as the vast bulk of Dexter swept by him. He sat absolutely still in the saddle, whilst Evelyn urged his mount on, gripping tightly with his legs, his body moving in concert with the gelding. Ned pulled his horse up in a disturbed state, its sides heaving, blood seeping from his nostrils. Fred urged his Irish mount on. As they approached the largest fence on the course, Dexter's chestnut loomed up on his outside. As they set their mounts at the jump, the portly banker appeared to lose a stirrup. As the horses took off, he grabbed at his mount's neck. Whilst Fred landed safely, Maximus pecked on landing. As if in slow motion, the horse somersaulted. Dexter was thrown forward, crashing to the ground, only to be submerged

for a second as the chestnut's impulsion sent him, legs flaying, over the prostrate jockey.
Fred was now ten lengths clear of the pursuing group, but Crowther was beginning to go to work on his mount. Evelyn was also making headway. Riding with shorter stirrups, his slender body hunched, he attacked the fences with a reckless disregard for either his or his horse's welfare. As they rounded the corner into the finishing straight Fred's horse made another mistake at the third last fence. Tiring, the horse missed its stride and ploughed through the birch. Fred's sheer strength stopped him from falling, but the horse had lost all its impetus. Distracted, Crowther's mount also made a mistake, and Evelyn moved up to join the others. The crowd was screaming. People were on there feet waving excitedly. I was stationed by the walkway leading back to the unsaddling enclosure. I could hear the hoof beats on the hard ground as they approached the second last. The three horses took off together. Again Fred Champion's mount stumbled, but he stayed on board. Crowther's filly also pecked on landing, but Evelyn flew the obstacle, riding with a demented energy. Fred was beaten. He eased his horse down, settling for third place. On the run-in to the last Crowther's filly was gaining. He sat still in the saddle, using just slight arm movements to urge the horse on. They were neck and neck. I found myself cheering for Evelyn. They took off in unison. Evelyn's mount hit the top of the jump, catapulting him head first, just yards from where I was standing. For a moment he lay quite still, whilst, ahead, Crowther raised his arms in victory. I ran over to help Evelyn as he rose uncertainly to his feet. He had a deathly pallor. His eyes were haunted, almost as if they had been set further back in his face. Retrieving his whip he lashed out at me, catching my arm, before staggering unsteadily into the watching crowds.
"Bad loser!" Fred Champion grinned down at me as I lead his sweating horse to the unsaddling enclosure, having finished a

distant second. Mr Fred dismounted and went off to weigh in. The groom placed a blanket over the gelding as we took the second berth in the winner's enclosure. It was then that I saw Kitty, leaning on the rail, reaching out trying to stroke the winner. I ran over to see what she had thought of the race. I don't know if she saw me or not, but she turned to walk off. I was about to shout after her when I realised that she was with a young man, who was vaguely familiar to me. She was laughing, smiling, her face upturned towards his. He slipped an arm around her waist. She willingly nestled into his shoulder. Crowds pushed past me, annoyed I was blocking their way. I stood my ground, watching the couple until they were out of sight.

* * * * * * * *

I am pleased to be travelling up to the Midlands by train. I find cars so uncomfortable now. Not that the first-class compartment is as I remember them. Only the different upholstery and carpets seem to distinguish them from standard-class. We are surrounded by serious-looking business executives. Most are young and all seem anxious to use their mobiles constantly. A few peer into laptop computer screens. No one uses the journey for enjoyment. There is not a book being read or even a crossword being undertaken. Intrusive call tones seem non-stop and conversations are conducted at an increasing pitch.

I am seated opposite Stephanie and she hands me a folder she has gathered from the archives. How have they managed to find so many shots? I am told that they will need a number of stills, to help illustrate parts of the programme not covered by existing film. She leaves me to browse whilst she goes off in search of coffee. The photographs don't appear to be in any particular order. Amazingly, they have been able to locate shots of me as a baby and a toddler. Most of the photographs cover my career from the good-looking youngster to the overweight, unhealthy-looking entertainer of the early fifties. There is a rather unflattering photo of my mother, taken at Champion House. Next I am pictured riding in Rotten Row with Lady Pamela Hornsby. No romance there, thank God! There are shots from the south of France, dear Noel Coward looking archly at me. Where did I get that ghastly swimming costume?

I'm not halfway through the pile and, frankly, I'm losing interest. I really don't care which shots they use. Then – there it is! In fact, there are two of them! I am stunned. I feel quite faint. I sense Stephanie returning, swaying down the corridor clutching the polystyrene cups. Instinctively, furtively, I slip the photographs into the pages of my newspaper. I need time to study them later, alone and without having to give an explanation. I have a feeling Stephanie saw me hide the photos, though she says nothing, and I'm sure my face shows guilt.

We have left London and the sprawling suburbs behind. Now fields stretch as far as the eye can see. My feelings are a mixture of excitement and apprehension.

At least the station at Stratton Market remains remarkably unchanged, a huge Victorian doll's house. I have looked forward to a drive through the town, but we turn left onto a new bypass. Within minutes we have left the busy road and are headed towards Theddington. I sit upright in my seat, looking for familiar landmarks. Approaching from the east the hall is the first property we will come to. The wall to the estate remains, protecting the house from prying eyes. Annoyingly, a cameraman films my reactions, from the front of the car. We swing right into the drive. The massive archway, bearing the Gibbs coat of arms, remains but the elms that used to line the drive have been uprooted.

"What is your first impression?" Stephanie asks. I don't reply. I am no longer the willing player in this game.

Sleeping policemen have been placed all the way up to the entrance. At first sight the hall looks very much the same as I remembered it, except the parkland and vegetable gardens have given way to fairways and rough. Men in baseball caps pulling trolleys and swishing clubs are dotted over the course. Women in smart, checked trousers practise their swings. We pull up outside the main entrance, which is now the reception area for the hotel. Painfully, I am released from the car. Stephanie helps me up the steep steps. The camera still homes in on me. Once more people stare. They probably think I'm some famous old golfer. Feeling in a truculent mood I pause and, turning, survey the course stretching into the horizon.
"What a waste; bloody stupid game; you would think people would find something better to do." With that little gem, I shuffle into reception. New partition walls and a false ceiling have robbed the area of its dramatic effect. They have blocked off the sweeping staircase, with its mahogany banisters, that drew the eye to the landing and the magnificent Guardi scene of St Mark's Square. A painting does remain, however. Too large for the reduced area, it is cramped above the original marble fireplace. Its presence is overbearing as the familiar face stares down at me. Evelyn Gibbs is captured in army uniform before he went to France. Presumably the present owners are not aware of the value of a work by Harold Knight. I am shocked by the expression on Evelyn's face. Surely my memory is playing tricks. I remember the young man being caught by the artist with a guileless grin, but now the face glowers down at me. He is angry that I have returned.

CHAPTER 11

I wasn't just jealous of Kitty for her increasing attractiveness to the opposite sex. It was more deep-rooted than that. Not long after she first started attending the grammar school the Curtis family moved to Stratton Market, where her parents seemed to be far happier. There were several other men who had brought home wives from foreign parts, and they were made more welcome than in the suspicious inward-looking atmosphere of a small village. Although I still saw Kitty regularly, particularly in her school holidays, she was forming a new circle of friends. The boy I saw with her at the races had been one of the stumbling lads I had noticed dancing self-consciously at Uppingham. She had become part of a group of intelligent and attractive friends, who although outwardly friendly towards me left me feeling excluded. Their conversation tended to be light-hearted and witty. I felt awkward and stupid in their company. For them the future was university and, with it, an array of opportunities.

I had already left school shortly after my 14th birthday. I had always struggled with my formal studies, although Miss Ormerod was disappointed by my departure. It was through Mrs Champion's influence that I joined Jepson's, the most exclusive of the five grocers in Stratton Market. For the next six years I was immersed in a grocery trade that was so different from today's market, dominated as it is by the huge supermarkets.

Jepson's occupied a favoured position, on the corner of the town's two main streets. I joined as an odd-job boy, but by the time I left for London I had risen to the post of under-manager. Mr Jepson was a man in his early fifties, who had taken the business on from his father and expanded it greatly. He decided that quality of service rather than price was the best way of attracting business. His strategy was successful, as he steadily acquired the orders of most of the local gentry, rather then having to compete for the popular end of the trade. The firm employed over 20 people, each grade distinguished by its uniform. The owner and manager wore black alpaca jackets, whilst the heads of department were dressed in short white coats with aprons reaching down to their shoes. Their aprons also had frilly edges, unlike those of the ordinary assistants, who had short aprons and crisply laundered shirts. There were four separate long, shiny mahogany counters, each overseen by their own staff. The bacon department alone employed two men, full-time. The abiding memory of the place was of smell. The wonderful aroma of coffee and tea competing with drying bacon. Each week coffee was roasted at the back of the shop. It was then ground and blended to each customer's requirements. There was very little pre-packaged food available. Everything had to be weighed and wrapped fresh. Over 30 blends of tea were available, to be measured from wooden chests. Sugar, butter and cheese were also all served in whatever quantity was required. There was a ritual and skill to the way in which each commodity was prepared, during which the customer sat at the counter on a high-backed stool watching or chatting to the owner.

I passed through the various departments as I grew older, graduating from the upstairs packing and assembling section to being made responsible for all the dried fruits that came into the shop. These arrived in huge, coarse sacks. The fruit firstly had to be washed and any stalks removed. Then came a second washing and the currants and sultanas were put through a sieve for grading. Finally they were washed with a syrupy water, to make the fruit look shiny and more appealing.

By the time I was 16 I was serving in the shop. Nothing was too much trouble. The smallest amount weighed and packaged with as much care as a large order. The customer was always right. I was helpful, sometimes cheeky, but

ultimately subservient. Butlers from the great houses were particularly important to the business. Nothing was too much trouble where they were concerned. I have a feeling Mr Jepson made them regular cash payments, to retain their business. Certainly, they were regularly invited into his office and the curtains would be drawn. It was not unusual to hear corks popping on these occasions. Wines were an important part of the trade and there were many refined palates to be satisfied locally.
My 18th birthday brought further promotion. I visited houses in surrounding villages, taking orders, all of which were delivered by motor transport, within 24 hours. All of my visits were made on a company bicycle and I was incredibly fit as I battled with the hills and inclines in all weathers. It was during this period that I became far more comfortable in ladies' company. I learnt how to flatter and flirt and yet cause no offence. It is only as you get older that you realise that very little of the experience you gain is wasted.

* * * * * * * *

Until Kitty started at the grammar school I had seen her almost every day since she moved into the village. Adolescence manifests itself in many ways. Some youngsters seem to reinvent themselves. Quiet, well-behaved young boys turn into rude, foul-mouthed teenagers. Some girls who have been plain in childhood suddenly blossom, whilst blonde-haired beauties at seven or eight turn into lumpy, taciturn young women. At first it was spots, erupting all over my face, that I thought were putting Kitty off me, but they disappeared as abruptly as they had arrived. I think, apart from my dullness at that time, it was my inability not to show my jealousy of her; of her quickness of thought, intelligence and ability to pass exams. I resented her new friends. I was jealous and hurt.

Perhaps it was the foreignness of her looks that attracted such a wide circle of admirers of both sexes. In rural England it was still rare to encounter people from outside the immediate area. I think Kitty worked out, very early, that her exotic looks could create real problems for her. Maybe it was her parents' influence; anyway, after an initial burst of short-lived boyfriends, she started to dress more conservatively and wearing her hair in a style that wasn't remotely stylish or very flattering. It was as if she was actively trying to postpone romantic interest in her. Even with shapeless frocks and a 'pudding basin' hairstyle it was impossible to disguise an amazing beauty that was refusing to be hidden. Someone meeting her for the first time would probably have taken her to be Italian or Spanish. She had an olive skin and thick, shiny black hair. Her features had fined down. The slightly chubby cheeks had retracted and now her high cheekbones, arched eyebrows and exquisite nose could present a look of aloofness on occasions. This would be eliminated the moment she smiled, with her sense of fun showing immediately. The whitest of teeth flashed, long eyelashes fluttered. She couldn't help it; there was no camouflage that could contain her overwhelmingly beauty.

Sometimes Kitty and her group of friends would turn up at a village dance where I was playing. Furtively I would watch her whilst I played, jealously noting whom she was dancing with. She and her friends were always complimentary about my playing. I felt they were patronising me. During a break from my playing a gramophone would normally blare out some of the hits of the day. I can never remember dancing with Kitty on these occasions. She would deflect me by suggesting I must need a drink or a rest, after all my efforts to entertain the dancers. This only increased my frustration with her, and I would go off in search of an attractive girl to dance with, in the hope of making Kitty jealous. She never even seemed to notice me.

Kitty did sometimes accompany me to the Globe cinema in Stratton Market, usually with at least one girlfriend. We must have been about 17 when my behaviour finally brought our friendship into real crisis. Many of the local girls had begun to think I was an attractive catch. I had a good regular job and was something of a local celebrity, with my emerging cabaret act. A number of breathless fumbling sessions behind village halls had increased my confidence. I was beginning to think I was irresistible. I was wrong!

For the first time that I could remember Kitty met me alone. I have no idea what film was showing; my mind was elsewhere. I tried to hold her hand in the dark, flickering light of the cinema. She took this advance to indicate I wanted some of the chocolates she was holding. Waiting for a few moments, I placed my arm around her shoulder. "Thanks," she whispered; "it is chilly in here," pretending it had been my intention to help her into her coat. In fact the cinema was warm and stuffy, so I decided to delay my advances to our walk home, to her house. My hopes rose as she agreed to take a short cut through the park. She was chatting away, seemingly unaware of my sense of anticipation. Taking her hand, I led her off the path and eased her up against the trunk of a huge elm. There was a partial moon and I mistook the look on her face to be one of suppressed longing, rather than concern. Taking her roughly in my arms I thrust myself against her, seeking her lips. She squirmed, turning her face from side to side.

"Bob!" Her voice was alarmed. "Don't; you're spoiling everything." She started to cry, and my passion subsided, in direct relation to my feeling of mortification. Still weeping, she led me by the hand to a park bench. Again I misread the signs. Putting my arms around her I drew her to me. "Kitty, can't you see I'm mad about you. I love you, for God's sake." She wiped the tears from her eyes. I could see her now, but I

couldn't understand her reaction. She seemed almost hysterical.
"Oh, Bob, I love you too. Of course I do."
"Well then."
"But not like that. Not that sort of love. You are my dearest friend; please don't ruin everything."
I protested. I even accused her of not wanting me because she thought I wasn't good enough. She was a snob, with all her grand friends. She thought I was stupid. She held my hands all the time I railed against her. Finally I could think of nothing more to say. I had made a fool of myself. There was a long silence. She continued to look at me with a strange expression on her face.
"Dear Bob. Don't be unhappy. I doubt if I shall ever love anyone more than I love you, but..."
"You think we are more like brother and sister, I suppose. Very convenient."
"No," she said. "Something quite different, but just as deep. I want us to continue as we were, but we must never..."
"Why?"
"Trust me. Please, it is so important."
"That's bloody rubbish; it's just an excuse. You think I'm too..."
She placed a cool finger over my lips. "Bob, I'm frightened."
"But Kitty, I've told you I love you."
"Please, let's pretend tonight never happened. You are going to be a great success one day and I will be proud to know you and still be your friend."
I began to protest, but she was desperate for me to agree that nothing had changed between us.
"Promise?" she asked, and sadly I nodded in agreement, but things had changed and we were never to rediscover the feelings of our childhood. I had ruined a part of our lives.

* * * * * * * *

My bedroom is in a modern annexe to the main building, connected by a long corridor with a hideous patterned carpet. The room smells of stale tobacco although it is in a non-smoking section of the hotel. It has all the facilities expected in a modern hotel room, but it is badly in need of renovation and redecoration. I turn the bed back. At least the linen looks clean.

Most of the production team have gone tenpin bowling, so I am to dine with Stephanie.

The clientele is almost entirely male and exclusively golfers. Separated from their loved ones for at least one night, they ogle Stephanie as she leads me to our table. Sorry chaps, you're wasting your time! The older men are the worst. Why do fat, bald-headed men become embarrassing lechers when they are let out for a night?

My arrival creates some interest as usual. Being old, you are sometimes made to feel that you have no right to venture out at all. The room is packed and I bump into the chairs of a couple of diners. Although seated well apart the men could be brothers. Cropped hair, huge bellies and an aura of aggression. The waitress is friendly, though, but the food dreadful. Beware menus with over-elaborate descriptions, cooked by chefs straight out of catering college. The whole place is depressing. It reflects what I feel about the country. Run-down and sad. Like the menu, we are sold a country and lifestyle in glowing terms. In reality, we endure poor services and constantly falling standards, underpinned by a thinly disguised air of aggression.

There is a grand piano, situated next to the dance floor. I ask Stephanie to excuse me. I start playing, but the hubbub of conversation continues. It is only when I start singing that quiet begins to descend. I give them *I can dream, can't I?*, followed by *Begin the beguine*. It is not an easy audience. There are a couple of rowdy guests, who think they are amusing. I am enjoying myself, though. The audience is now under my control. The applause grows louder. I am on my fourth encore when I see that Stephanie has managed to find the cameraman. I am showing off now. *You go to my head*, I croon. The chefs have appeared from the kitchens and the waitresses have stopped clearing the tables. I finish and bow. The applause is deafening. Just one last number, then. With no sense of foreboding I give them *You stepped out of a dream*.

* * * * * * * *

Once again I fight sleep. It is made easier for me by a party that seems to be taking place in the next room. I almost welcome the drunken laughter. Eventually they all say goodnight and the place is quiet at last. Several times I start, as if someone has walked over my grave. I open my eyes, only for an overwhelming tiredness to engulf me. I can fight it no more.

Incredibly, I am suspended above what appears to be a football stadium. The high-banked stands are full to overflowing and many of the crowd have spilled out onto the pitch. The playing surface is not marked out. In fact, it has no grass. The earth is dry and dusty. The crowd is excitable. I can tell because they are clapping their hands and waving, but there is no sound.

Now my attention is drawn to the centre of what should be the playing area. A huge pyre has been erected, rising to the height of some 20 feet. Three men dressed in flowing orange robes are carrying a shroud of white cotton. The body enclosed is stiff and unwieldy. I don't want to watch. I feel uneasy, but I am fascinated. The body is lashed to a central pole with coarse ropes. The crowd have surged forward now, climbing over crash barriers and fences to get a closer view. A figure in a black gown wields a long knife theatrically above his head, then, bending, he starts slitting the shroud, first exposing the ankles of the corpse.

I feel as if I am still awake, but the images persist. I feel myself thrashing about.

The knife continues upwards, exposing white, wasted, obscene limbs. I feel bile rising in my throat. The shroud falls away. The pyre has been lit. My legs are soaked. I can feel my pyjamas warm against my skin. The cadaver smiles up at me. I know that smile. I should do – it's mine!

Now the crowd parts and she comes towards me. She wears a fixed smile as she approaches the smouldering pyre. I want to warn her, but there is not a pause in her step. I try to shout. Silence. She walks into the flames. I can smell singeing hair. She reaches out for me. The flames lick hungrily round me. I am burning. My flesh is becoming blackened. I am petrified, revolted. I scream. I am lying on the floor; my hip aches. I am crying. Sobbing like a baby. I have had enough – I want to die. Outside I can hear a chambermaid hoovering the hideous patterned carpet.

CHAPTER 12

Shakily I draw back the curtains and open the window. It is still quite dark outside. The air is icy. For a moment it cools my sweating body. Then, suddenly, I am shaking, with cold now rather than fear, and I shut the elements out again. The chambermaid continues her noisy journey down the corridor. It's not seven o'clock yet!

I must ring Maria. I need some comfort – a familiar voice. The night porter takes an age in giving me a line. His voice is effeminate and abrupt. He is annoyed. I have interrupted whatever he was doing. The line is engaged. Who can she be talking to at this time of the day? I keep on trying, but the line doesn't clear. My reaction is out of all proportion. Tears well up in my eyes. My heart is fluttering, I have a headache, I feel sick. I lower my pyjama trousers; deep bruising is already etching its way across my hip, following my fall.

Lying on the bed I pull the covers over me and reach for the photographs I ghosted away on the train. These have a calming effect almost immediately. Struggling with my glasses I am transported back across the years. How extraordinary that this moment, above all others, should have been captured, and yet I had no idea.

I sit at my piano with Tilly Nash, a hand on my shoulder, the other decorously clasping a slender cigarette holder. A wisp of smoke from her Balkan Sobranie is frozen in time. Tilly stares rather accusingly upwards. Several of the diners also glance to the top of the curving staircase. There, accompanied by the head waiter, is Kitty. I don't appear to have noticed her yet, but I remember the tension transmitted by Tilly's hand that, seconds later, caused me to catch sight of my childhood friend for the first time in almost two years. I think in that very moment both Tilly and I realised our six-month relationship was at an end.

The old black and white photo conveys only a fraction of the atmosphere created by that amazing entrance. Now it looks almost fake, stage-managed. The composition is too perfect and yet it goes some way to recreating an elegant age that has altogether vanished. Even without knowing any of the cast, it represents a piece of social history. There are jewels and long gloves, chandeliers and starched shirts. Potted palms, long hock glasses, haughty stares, attentive waiters, fur stoles, slicked-down hair – and Kitty. I move the photograph so the beam from my bedside light shines directly on her. She wears a rather embarrassed expression and yet, even now, I cannot believe that she was unaware of the impact she was making. She has just removed the veil from her face. Her thick black hair falls in cascades to below her shoulders. Her sari, I remember, was of a brilliant blue: a colour I have witnessed only on the subcontinent. The fabric was relieved with floral motifs, etched in gold, and round her waist and on the short sleeves of her sari pearls were looped. Her midriff was bare and on her feet she wore gold, open-toed sandals. The second photograph must have been taken moments later. I have stopped playing. More people have turned to stare. Tilly looks angry. She appears to be talking to me. I don't hear a thing. I am caught, rising from my stool; I still remember my feelings at that moment. It is as if I have been hit in the pit of the stomach. Our eyes are locked onto each other. She looks less assured than in the previous shot. I have a feeling of sudden elation.

I was certain, at that very moment, that I was about to be released from my fake world of casual liaisons and empty enjoyment.

The shrill ring of the telephone interrupts my thoughts. It's Maria. She demands to know why I haven't rung her. She is cross. Have I been taking my pills? What time is my flight arriving? I am vague. I feel rather disorientated. The voice

that a few minutes before I had longed to hear hangs up on me.
"Stupid woman!" I splutter angrily. My voice sounds different, as if I am speaking with a mouthful of cotton wool. Laboriously I struggle into my dressing grown and sit on a stained armchair to watch the dawning of a new day. My room looks over the terrace where once Sir Percy took afternoon tea, but which now is lined with golf trolleys. They are set out with an almost military precision. Through a chill mist I can make out the wood-clad professionals' shop and, beyond, the outline of the greenkeeper's sprawling tin workshop.
The day is grudging in revealing itself. Darkness gives way to swirling mist, which allows tantalising glimpses of the landscape before being eaten up again. It is still over an hour to breakfast, so I decide to get dressed and have a walk before too many people are about. I'm beginning to feel a little better. I wrap up well, encased in woollen underwear, shirt and waistcoat, and topped by my overcoat with the astrakhan collar, Burberry scarf and fedora.
The newspapers are being sorted by the night porter as I make my way across the reception area. He is a small man with dyed black hair combed forward over his forehead. His manner is high camp and he complains loudly to no one in particular about the lack of help he is receiving. Two receptionists giggle together further down the counter. I feel his performance is for the girls' amusement. "Where's my *Telegraphs*?" he pouts; "too many *Suns* and no *Telegraphs*. Oh well, it's tits for everyone at breakfast, poor things." The girls dissolve into hysterics and I tentatively brace the elements.
Outside I try to get my bearings. I have the rather macabre idea that I want to visit the lake again. Why? What can it reveal after all these years? I peer through the gloom from the putting green, which is covered in a thin film of frost. As a

child the lake didn't seem far away from the house, but it's probably the best part of a mile. I would duck and weave through the bracken and undergrowth, anxious to leave the darkness of the wood and never failing to wonder at the beauty of the clearing leading down to the water's edge, particularly in the spring, when I trod gently over a carpet of swaying bluebells and daffodils.
An outlandish figure appears from the gloom. His hair is gelled into a series of spikes, each of a different colour. He wears what appears to be curtain rings hanging from his ears.
"You alright, grandad? You'll catch your death standing out here."
He is cheeky. 'Cocky' we would have called him in my day, but he has a friendly face and a wicked smile. He is a member of the greens staff and I explain that I used to live in the village and knew the house when it was privately owned. I ask him if the lake is still in existence.
"Too right," he informs me; "the 14th – bugger of a hole. The most difficult par three on the course." He offers to take me over on a golf buggy, as he has some work to do on a couple of adjoining greens. He is very patient, helping me into the unfamiliar vehicle and then running back to his workshop to bring a coarse blanket to cover my legs. I am confused by the young. They tend to look so dreadful and yet, on balance, they seem more caring than my contemporaries at their age.
Two rakes rattle behind us in the section of the buggy where golf bags are usually stowed. He drives the battery-powered vehicle with an extravagant expertise. A watery sun threatens to pierce the grey clouds before silently submitting to the overall gloom. My companion whistles tonelessly as we squelch down sodden fairways. I hang on tight as we skid down north-facing slopes, still covered in a thin white frost. The mist swirls, thickening as we progress. I sense rather than see our approach to the water's edge. My breath comes in shallow intakes, accompanied by several alarming cackles

from my lungs. The air has a pungency. My eyes are watering. I must cut a pathetic figure. The young man glances at me and skids the buggy down a final steep hill where the frost is turning to water as I watch.

I can make out the water's edge now, further down a muddy slope. My young friend suggests that I stay put whilst he goes off to rake neighbouring bunkers. I tell him I shall keep warmer on the move. He looks doubtful and insists on wrapping the blanket round my shoulders. It smells of engine oil and is harsh to the touch. He disappears into the mist, assuring me he will be back within ten minutes.

I totter precariously down the bank and try to pierce the mist in the direction of where the boathouse used to stand. There is total silence but for the gentle lapping of the water, and yet there is no breeze. Not a breath of air. I am alone in a world bounded by the swirling mist. All I can see are a few bulrushes and the sad winter leaves of water lilies. I screw up my eyes, peering, as if by willpower I can somehow cut through the fog. I am aware how stupid I must look. How stupid I am, standing in a frozen field, seeking something that no longer exists. And yet, as ever, this place exerts a strange hold over me.

I can't remember if I lose my footing or just walk into the water. Memories, fact, fiction and dreams all seem interlinked. I am unable to decipher one from the other. At first a cold shaft runs through my entire body, but soon the water appears almost comforting. I am in a trance-like state, aware that I am wading out into deeper water and yet prompted by a compulsion of familiarity and nearness. The mist is gradually receding, although it remains murky. Am I going mad? Now the sun seems to be setting rather than rising. I sense myself start, as I stare uncomprehendingly across the lake as I remembered it from my youth. There on its far bank is the stilted boathouse, its paint still peeling, the balcony rails broken. I gulp in a deep breath, for there on that dangerous platform stands Kitty. I want to shout out to her, but I am mute. I wade forward, waving frantically. The water has reached my waist and I am stumbling over rocks and getting caught up in weed. I think Kitty has heard me. She is looking round. I can see her clearly now, full face. God, she is gorgeous. My heart lurches crazily. She looks frightened, alarmed even. "Don't worry," I shout in my head, "it's only me; I'm coming."

Her distress only heightens her beauty. Her hair is drawn back in the way I love to see it. She wears the green, sleeveless cotton dress she wore when I took her shopping in London, simple and yet so elegant. I feel a huge surge of emotion. We are to be together again.

Suddenly she runs inside the boathouse, slamming the double doors behind her. The grubby windows I remember are broken now, just a few jagged edges remaining, enabling me to catch glimpses of her as she dashes for the entrance. She must have seen me after all. I feel tears of joy well up and I push on deeper into the water. My attention is drawn to a light, flickering on the path approaching the boathouse. The sun has dipped behind the trees. I can make out a lamp being carried by an indistinct figure, hurrying forward. Kitty is now standing on the rickety steps to the entrance. She stands motionless, a hand held to her mouth. Like a rabbit caught in a car's headlights, she appears incapable of moving. The paraffin lamp dances on its metal handle, but the figure rushing forward is still obscured from me. For the first time I feel a sense of alarm. Kitty must too, for she turns, but her shoe gets caught in one of the rotting slats. She pauses before abandoning the shoe and moving swiftly back into the boathouse and shutting the door. Inside, she appears to be trying to wedge a chair under the door handle.

The lamp continues to swing, held in a strong hand as the figure bounds up the rotting stairs. I try to yell, shout, cry a warning, but I am speechless. A pewter crucifix bounces against a heaving chest. There are beads of sweat on his face. His long hair looks wet in the half-light. With two mighty kicks the door splinters and the chair is sent spinning. Kitty struggles with the doors onto the balcony. She twists at the handle, glancing nervously over her shoulder. Now she is out on the disintegrating balcony. She sucks in air. She is about to jump. She is a strong swimmer. Jump, my darling, jump! He is upon her. Roughly he pulls her back into the building. He is kissing her. This is intolerable. Kitty tries to fight him off. They stagger like a couple of drunks. The lamp falls from my view. He forces her across the room. He is pinioning her to the wall. He is a madman! My brain shrieks with rage.

There is a glow coming from the building, heightened as darkness closes in outside. I can see Kitty plainly now. He is thrusting at her, stumbling along the wall as she tries to fight him off. How dare he – a man of the cloth! Her struggling becomes even more demented. She is warning him of danger as she stares with a petrified expression over his shoulder. He is out of control. His hands are all over her body. The whoosh of the small explosion does attract his attention. Within seconds the glow becomes an inferno. The place is a tinderbox. Sparks fly, wood crackles and spits. As he stands back, I can see he has torn her lovely dress.

The entrance is now fully alight. Forks of fire lick their way towards the ceiling. He rushes towards the balcony. The doors he had slammed violently as he dragged Kitty into the building are stuck. He charges at them, but stubbornly they refuse to give. He glances down and screams in horror. His cassock has caught fire. He dances a demented tango, trying to extinguish the flames. Kitty looks on. I swear she is laughing at him – or is she crying? I try to move closer. He takes her in his arms again. This time he is not prompted by lust, he seems to seek her protection. He appears to squeal for help as the flames spread up his back. With one last violent lunge he pulls her to the floor; there they roll like children playing, in an attempt to put out the flames. The glass in the photographs lining the walls cracks before crashing to the floor. The giant telescope glows, as if a dedicated housemaid has spent hours cleaning the brass, before slowly it wavers, toppling onto its side. The lens disintegrates, leaving a dark aperture, like an empty eye socket. Finally there is noise. I can hear the fire consuming the old building, and even from the distance feel its heat. Then, with the utmost clarity, I hear Kitty's voice.

"Mitch," she calls; "oh, Mitch." It is not a voice of alarm, nor even a cry for help. It is the whisper of a lover.

Then I am at peace again. A feeling of warmth and comfort. I am vaguely aware of thinking: "This is it, then." Death is a welcome retreat from a troubled world and dark memories. Then, a violent explosion in my mind and lungs. Strong arms are tearing at my shirt, ripping off the buttons at my throat. Water spouts from my month, hands hammer my back. More water, bile, and then air. Painful air trying to get to my lungs. Peace returns for a moment, then there are lips on mine. Unfamiliar lips, a sour taste of cigarette smoke. I sense they are male lips. Even at this moment I am revolted. I struggle, but the foul breath is being blown into my reluctant lungs. I feel a huge eruption within me. It catapults me forward and I spew lake water all over my rescuer. I hear him blaspheme. I am vaguely aware of him talking, calling for help on his mobile. I pass in and out of consciousness; opening my eyes I am aware of people towering above me as I lie on the damp grass. I think I can hear Stephanie's voice, but before I can focus I glimpse a hypodermic needle.

* * * * * * * *

The white-coated doctor insists I must stay in hospital for at least two days whilst they undertake tests. I am dismissive.

What good are test at my age, for goodness' sake? Stephanie appears shaken by the incident at the lake, as if in some way she is responsible.
She has become increasingly protective towards me. She says I should return to Spain as soon as possible. She reckons she has enough film in the can to complete the programme. I didn't want to come to Theddington in the first place, but 'the show must go on' is deeply engrained in me. So, 24 hours after almost drowning, I discharge myself from Stratton General.
Stephanie throws me anxious glances as she drives me back to the hotel. I do feel pretty peaky. It is as if a cheese grater has been forced down my throat. I am certainly weak, but I can bear a day's shooting in the village and then a final short session in Stratton Market tomorrow morning. Stephanie has booked me a flight to Malaga from Birmingham, so within 48 hours I shall be back in Maria's loving care.
Filming is not due to take place until after lunch. I have coffee with Stephanie and then walk over to the greenkeeper's workshop to thank the young man who plucked me from the water. It's a lovely morning; quite mild, with pale winter sunshine. I haven't really had time to think about my experience at the lake. It all seemed so real, but the doctor explained at great length that immersion in water can prompt all manner of illusions. I didn't bother to tell him that I'm sure I witnessed most of the horrifying events before being submerged.
I bang on the green metal door and enter. The workshop is long, dark and cluttered. A tractor jacked up on bricks and minus a tyre obscures my view. There is a strong smell of petrol and acrid chemicals. "Hello!" I call out. The figure at the far end is hunched over a tabloid paper, eyes strained under a flickering fluorescent light. "Can you help me? I'm looking for the young lad with the spiky hair."

"Darren's not here, sir. Hey, aren't you the gentleman he pulled out of the lake?"
He continues to enquire as to how I am. I feel myself shaking again as if I have just been pulled from the water. I grab the tractor to stop myself falling. Rudely I interrupt him. "Where did you get that?"
He smiles, fingering the leather thong at his neck. "What, this? My missus hates it. Cool, though, don't you reckon?"
"Not the leather, the…" I can't even bring myself to say it.
"Bit rusty, like."
"Where did you get it?" I am shouting; the greenkeeper looks quite shocked. I don't really need to hear his answer, I know where it has come from.
"We clear the lake once a year to collect all the lost balls. Nice little earner, I can tell you! Found it last year. Local antique dealer says it's made of pewter. Not worth much, though."
I turn and make my way towards the thin shaft of light at the end of the workshop.
"By the way," he calls after me, "the antiques bloke reckons it ain't English. Greek Orthodox crucifix it is, according to him. You alright, sir?"

CHAPTER 13

The *Stratton Market Gazette*, April 21st 1931.

The Stratton Hunt Ball, held at the Assembly Rooms

Most of the country houses in the neighbourhood were represented and there were many visitors from across the country.
The stewards were: Viscount Deane, Sir Richard Amery, Sir Percy Gibbs and Mr J Templeton-Knight.
The decorations were charming. The hall lends itself to being transformed into a fine ballroom. The decorators made the most of the opportunity and achieved remarkable results. Streamers of green and white were suspended from the centre of the ceiling to the cornices. The walls were draped with the same colours, and at intervals large mirrors were placed with flower boxes at their base. In the recesses were handsome ormolu gerondoles, lighted with candles and ornamented by pretty shades. The area was bordered with rich carpets, upon which was placed beautiful antique furniture.
Underneath, the balcony was tastefully furnished for sitting out. Handsome chairs and settees had been placed on oriental carpets. The platform to the bandstand was beautifully bordered with flowering plants and its walls draped with gold-brocaded silk curtains. The corners to the stage were lined with groups of palms.
The lobby at the east end of the hall was furnished in crimson satin and was utilised as a tearoom. This in turn led on to the small hall, which was used as a supper room. A sumptuous buffet was laid on, comprising cold meats, roasted fowl, pies from Melton Mowbray and Scottish salmon. Wines included vintage champagnes, clarets from the leading vineyards and a selection of white wines from the Loire. An array of fruit

cups were also available. The lavish food was supplied by Messrs Gunter and sons of Berkeley Square, London.
Music was by Clifford Heywood and his band to a strict programme of waltzes, foxtrots and gavottes. At the repeated requests of some of the larger parties attending, some modern American numbers were added. It is doubtful if any previous Stratton Ball had witnessed such uninhibited enjoyment on the dance floor.
Interval entertainment also concentrated on the modern vogue. Local performer Robert Mitchell received a standing ovation for his rendition of popular songs of the moment, including: *Time on my hands*, *Just one more chance*, and *If I had a talking picture of you*. It was noticeable that few revellers took the opportunity to dine until Mr Mitchell's performance was concluded. This correspondent understands that Mr Harold Goldman, a leading London impresario, who was a guest of Mr & Mrs William Champion of Champion House, has offered young Mr Mitchell an opportunity to pursue a professional career under his guidance. We shall watch Mr Mitchell's progress with interest.
It was gone one o'clock before the distinguished gathering started their homeward journey. Passing through the deeply carpeted entrance hall, and protected from a light rain by the huge striped awning, their chauffeurs jostled for position in the latest examples of luxury motorised transport. The whole evening was deemed to have been a true success.

* * * * * * * *

This is the only press cutting I have kept, from a career covering four decades. Faded now by time, and fraying where the paper has been folded for over 70 years, the article has survived unscathed from its immersion in the lake, protected by the plastic folder that also holds my credit cards.

Whilst I remember being elated by the reaction to my performance that night, I so wished Kitty had been there to witness my success. She hade gone up to medical school in Edinburgh, some two years previously. Although she came home regularly I missed her with an intensity that only the young can muster. We exchanged letters on an almost weekly basis. She appeared to be totally absorbed by her medical studies and what I assumed to be the rarefied life of a leading university. My letters with tales of local gossip, village dances and the bacon counter seemed dull even to me. At least my breakthrough at the hunt ball provided my first really exciting news and her response was so warm and open. I was still aware that a certain reserve had built up between us. I knew I was responsible and that it dated back to my making such a clumsy pass at her. Nonetheless, I felt unable to be completely natural and at ease in her company when she did return home.

On each of these visits I looked for a change in her attitude towards me, but if anything she became more remote. I was still smitten; she seemed more beautiful, even mysterious, each time we met. She was rarely alone during these short breaks. She tended to be surrounded by her old grammar school friends, or fellow students that she had met at medical school. I was hopelessly lovesick, and it must have been obvious, because my mother started teasing me. Kitty was certainly friendly. Almost too friendly. She was jolly when I wanted to talk seriously, and formal when I just longed for us to have fun together. I realise now she was keeping me at an emotional arm's length.

Looking back, my love for her never changed, other than in its intensity. From a childhood friendship, when we were inseparable, to a longing for her, when I was a young man, that was sidelined early on. Then it lay, seemingly dormant, until we met again years later, from where it rampaged, out of control, only to be cut short so tragically. Even now, after I

am dismantling the walls of my selective memory, my love for her haunts and taunts me still.
I know I must return to what happened at the lake, but only when I'm calmer. Did I really witness all those images or do I have an over-imaginative mind? Was it just an extension of a whole series of frightening images or am I finally going soft in the head?

* * * * * * * *

After a snack lunch I am driven to where Champion House used to stand. Now it's an executive housing estate. Expensive houses, yet their external walls only a few inches apart. Each construction is slightly different in design from its neighbour, but laid out in theme. Elizabethan Way is given over to mock-Tudor design, whilst Georgian Avenue features double-glazed sash windows and porticoes. The unifying factor is huge garages, enough in most instances to house three cars. Presumably the majority of the breadwinners are at work, but there is still a fair scattering of BMWs, Mercedes and Japanese four-wheel drive models. Everything is immaculate; tidy lawns and raked gravel drives. This is the English version of those sweeping estates so often featured in American films. Smaller in scale, prissy, but espousing the virtue of having made something out of life and showing it. Clusters of women, some with young children, gather, intrigued by the cameramen and production crew.
The Champions' business had apparently continued to expand right through the war, bolstered once more by lucrative government contracts. As corsets fell from favour, the company diversified into swimwear. In common with much of the British textile trade, however, the business started to contract, and by the end of the sixties the group was confined to its original factory in Stratton Market. By the early seventies matters were becoming critical, and the family sold

out to one of the few remaining British giants. Now there is not a single Champion listed in the local phone book. What would old William Champion have thought? All that industry, planning and scheming. For what? As for his wife, the grand and unpredictable Lettice, I doubt if that couple, to whom I owed so much, would have skulked away with a soft pay-off, whatever the trading conditions. They would have fought, used their nous, to be a step or two ahead of the opposition. Presumably their direct descendants were still living in some comfort, having taken the easy option.

Some of the giant Scottish pines that surrounded the old house remain. They thrust skyward, uneasy in their new environment, somehow out of place. It is difficult to get my bearings, but now, over latticed wooden fences, I see a familiar outline. The stable block has been left; or, rather, redeveloped into mews flats. I am filmed as I walk gingerly through the arch and stare up at the rooms where I lived with my mother all those years ago. Now there is no smell of sweating horses or dry hay. Satellite dishes cling to the old walls. The quadrangle, where the grooms used to dry off the horses after a day's hunting, is covered now in immaculate gravel. Hanging baskets and window boxes attempt to create an atmosphere in kilter with the surrounding countryside, and yet somehow the apartments would be more in keeping with Islington or Hampstead.

I'm asked about my time here. I'm feeling uncooperative. I would like to be alone with my thoughts. The filming is interminable. I have an urge to be outrageous on camera, but I just manage to control myself. I am struck by the fact that here is a perfect example of how things have changed in my lifetime. Once privilege ran alongside poverty. A world where servants could be hired or dismissed on a whim. Now, replaced by a society where the majority are far better off. And yet, is the quality of life better? I suppose it's natural for an old man to look back nostalgically, to days that have assumed an almost mythical warmth. I can wrap myself in the comfort of my childhood, but other harsher memories keep intruding. Eventually we are done here. We can leave the executives' wives to their school runs. To their tidy gardens, custom-built computer rooms, and state-of-the-art kitchens.

The main street in the village is unrecognisable even from my last visit here, some 30 years ago. There had been huge changes even then, from my memories as a young man. A garage had been built where once the abattoir had stood. The village school was empty and neglected. Functional shops, those required for everyday living, remained, but for the most part run by newcomers. Since then, the village had been transformed again. The imposing church is about the only building that looks unchanged. Symbolic, somehow. Whilst, over hundreds of years, it has dominated the village, all around it was in a constant state of decline or renewal. Perhaps my lifelong aversion to religion was wrong. Was the truth represented by this place of worship, its spire still thrusting to the heavens, steadfast, immovable, in the face of accelerating change?

Stratton Market has spread its tentacles, so now there is hardly a break from its outposts to the sign indicating entry into Theddington. Stratton is now a maze of housing estates encircling the old town. The village signpost is important, however. For on the Theddington side live the ambitious, the achievers or the dreamers with huge mortgages. The corrugated iron roofs of my childhood have been replaced with Collyweston tiles or new golden thatch. Expensive dress shops, estate agents and smart restaurants line the street. The wool shop run by mad Mrs Morris is now a branch of Barclays Bank. No closures here; too much money about! There are traffic wardens, and yet Range Rovers still park on double yellow lines. This is Burberry and green welly country. I can see rolling fields beyond the houses, but no farm workers shop or live here any more.

Next we film inside the church. A young vicar beams as I recount the story of my father's outburst on his return from the war. I keep it simple, not elaborating. Even the church has altered. Although it had always been well endowed, it retains a certain starkness that I remember from my youth. Now huge wall heaters beat down, taking away the musty smell of dampness. The altar has been enlarged, encroaching into the body of the church, presumably because congregations are so small. The vicar tells me he is responsible for three parishes and that he lives in a small semi down in Stratton.

We move onto where I spent the first seven years of my life. Curiosity is my overriding emotion, rather than trepidation, as we enter the building. The property had been sold back in the eighties and it is now an antique shop. I am no expert, but it appears to me that much of the stock is either over-restored or reproduction. Everything is beautifully set out. The furniture is small and shiny, suitable for compact modern homes. The pictures are mainly prints, in modern frames, whilst the copper and brass have the look of Far Eastern imports. There are some genuine pieces dotted about. I find the prices listed quite staggering.

Amidst all the clutter it is difficult for me to get my bearings. Walls have been demolished, to form a huge open showroom downstairs. I pick my way between reproduction pub mirrors and a table lined with Staffordshire figures, to the side of the building where we used to have our rooms. It's an intense disappointment to me that I am quite unable to recreate in my mind the old kitchen and small living room. How many hours did I spend watching my mother knit and sew? How often did I sit on her lap, as she patiently helped me to read and spell? Have I really, somewhere within this mutilated room, been cuddled and scolded? I feel cheated and annoyed by the changes.

Perhaps this is why I take such a dislike to the proprietor. He is a man in his fifties and he seems to me to be as fake as his stock. His accent, for a start! I am an expert on accents – I know an impostor when I meet one! After all, I had good money spent on me, ironing out my flat vowels. He alternates between arrogance and obsequiousness. The fawning side is apparent when he is on film. Off camera he lets us know we are something of a bloody nuisance. It is with the greatest of difficulty that he is persuaded to let us look upstairs. He wants us to film his bedroom, the same one where years before Beresford Egan had slept. He is rather thrown as we move to the back of the house. My mother's room. For a short period, my parents' bedroom. At last I am able to connect with my surroundings. I can ignore the jumble, the unmade bed. The familiar view from the window. The same mean, tiled fireplace. I ask for a rickety modern dressing table to be moved. There the door into the eaves remains exactly as I remembered it.

Stephanie senses my change of mood and asks me what the significance of the cupboard door is. I lie. I tell her nothing and filming is stopped.

Downstairs Lawrence Butterworth, the shop's owner, makes a great performance in presenting me with a scrapbook that he has purchased recently. He tells the camera that it covers events in the village, with items dating back to Victorian times. He hands it over to me with his compliments. It is a huge leather-bound book, the spine of which has broken and some of the pages jut out. As we leave I see Stephanie handing him a wad of notes.

"Some gift," I say. She smiles ruefully and tells me she is still well within budget for the programme. "Typical antique dealer," she complains, "he wouldn't take a cheque." I feel quite guilty, because it was Stephanie who thought I would like the album, as a sort of memento. The book weighs heavily on my knee and she takes it from me. I am feeling very tired and ask to be excused from a special supper she has arranged for me and the crew. She looks concerned and asks if I am alright. I nod. She holds my hand as we sweep up the drive to the hotel. I feel strangely comforted by her concern. I wish she would stay with me, holding my hand as I try to go to sleep. Just as my mother had done when I was a child. I dare not ask her. She wouldn't understand. I squeeze her hand very tight. She senses my unease. "Don't worry, it's almost over now," she says.

CHAPTER 14

I don't feel too guilty about missing the final night's party with the production team. They will have a better time without me. The thought of spending a quiet evening on my own, even in this bleak room, is so appealing. A time for reflection. I think, on balance, I was wrong to sanction the programme in the first place. One thing that doesn't decline with age is ego. I still enjoy being the centre of attention. Pathetic, really!

My memory is an increasing problem. Some events so vivid, and yet vast empty tracts predominate. Where do memories end and imagination take over? For some reason it is the sad or tragic events that remain etched in my mind. Yet there *were* good times.

The summer of 1932 is now something of a haze, but what memories I do retain are of a time of excitement and change. This was to be my period of apprenticeship. Harry Goldman had booked me solidly from May through to the beginning of October, touring the south coast. I was to start in Cornwall, gradually travelling east, before ending my tour in Brighton. Fat Man Filkins departed to Paris and it was left to the girls to give me a suitable send-off. Before leaving I was fitted up for two tail suits and a smart white tuxedo, which I was instructed to reserve for particularly warm nights. My hair was restyled at Toppers, in Jermyn Street. I was sent to a leading theatrical photographer in Denman Street. Flattering shots were taken of me, in profile, using shadow to clever effect by fining down my somewhat coarse features. "I love your chin," the photographer told me, "and your lips – very sensual." He was not in the least effeminate, but as he tilted my head this way and that his hands caressed my face. Perhaps he could sense in me the sexual release that Bea had unleashed – but not for my own sex, thank you!

I can't remember how many girls I frequented before travelling down to Cornwall; certainly, all my early experiences were with the trade. Without exception they all told me to find myself a proper girlfriend. Some charged me a normal amount, others half price. A few made fun of me, laughing openly at my fevered attempts. With Bea, though, it was altogether more intense. She was a tough nut, insisting that I pay her, and yet I was sure that she used our sessions to abandon herself to a world in which she imagined I was a true lover. At times I found the experience quite frightening, but she would soon recover, calling me 'a clumsy oaf'. It was she who taught me to be a sensitive and skilful lover. I think the money was well spent, unless the countless ladies in my life were better actresses than I took them to be.

After a drunken farewell party in the Dog and Duck, I counted nine of the girls waving me off at Paddington station. They tottered on their high heels, shouting out comments that had my fellow passengers hiding behind their newspapers. As the train drew off, grunting and straining, filling the air with acrid smoke, it was Bea who set off first for the taxi rank. She was dabbing her eyes with a handkerchief. At that moment I felt very alone and frightened. I was travelling to a world about which I knew nothing and felt ill prepared.

I was met at Truro station by a hotel car driven by a uniformed chauffeur. He seemed unsure how to address me. He obviously knew I was some kind of entertainer, but I think it was my age that caused his difficulty. That and my cheap suitcase, yet expensive flannels and blazer. The word 'sir', when addressing me, seemed to stick in his throat. I was aware of his dark brooding eyes, surveying me from his driving mirror.

Much of that summer I stayed in theatrical digs, but at the Castle Hotel I was allotted one of the rooms normally allocated for guests' chauffeurs. The hotel was a vast Victorian pile, much favoured by affluent families from the

shires. The public rooms and bars were comfortable, rather than fashionable. Leather sofas, upholstered easy chairs and fires lit daily even during fine spells. The grounds had walks down to the beach along wood-lined paths. There were several lawn tennis courts and an immaculate croquet lawn.
My own room was small and sparsely furnished. It was clean, though, with a comfortable bed. Like the chauffeur, the staff didn't know quite how to react to me. I was informed by the manager that I could have breakfast with guests in the dining room, whilst other meals were to be taken in the staff hall. I never did make it down to breakfast. I had already become accustomed to retiring late and sleeping well into the morning. My posed photograph was displayed outside the dining room, along with the evening's menu. The caption read simply: 'Mitch Entertains'. I spent ages that first evening getting myself ready. Ignoring the hammering on the staff bathroom door, I lay back covered in suds, going through my routine in my head. Although not normally nervous, my first professional appearance was so important and I felt very vulnerable. Somehow I had expected Mr Goldman, or a member of his staff, to witness my first night, but nobody had made themselves known to me. I sauntered back to my room, wrapped just in a towel, dripping water onto the linoleumed floor. Two chambermaids peered round their bedroom door giggling, until a blood-curdling voice shouted, "Cover yourself up, boy."
Mrs Armitage, the housekeeper, must have been fat at some stage in her life, for her clothes hung off her and her jowls sagged and wobbled as she spoke.
"We know all about you London types," she said accusingly. I informed her I wasn't from London. "Theatrical types, then." We were, according to her, a danger to all God-fearing folk. I skulked back to my room, her tirade still in full flow as I closed the door.

My opening night was a huge anticlimax. The hotel was barely half full and I had completed my first three numbers before anyone seemed to notice me. One large table was taken up by sober-suited businessmen. They were directors of the local building society, who had just held their annual general meeting. The other diners, mostly elderly, were scattered throughout the sizeable room, rarely raising their gaze from their plates. My training in involving the audience into my act didn't apply. The diners were all seated well away from me. By the time I had finished my first session I was convinced I was the victim of a conspiracy. I had been placed far too close to the kitchen, and waiters constantly clattered dishes and obscured my view.

After a short break my second stint was even worse. Although it was only just after nine o'clock, the dining room had almost emptied. I threw everything into my routine, drawing some desultory applause from an elderly couple of ladies as they prepared to leave. By the time I reached my final number there was not even a member of staff left in the room. A huge feeling of disappointment overwhelmed me. This was not what I expected. As I made my way back to the staff quarters, the lights in reception were already being turned off. Taking off my bow tie and loosening the restricting collar stud, I realised I didn't feel remotely tired, and yet there was nowhere for me to go. As I tramped down the corridor to my room, a door opened, preceded by giggles. Two young girls, one a waitress that I had noticed in the dining room, thrust a book in front of me and asked for my autograph. This was the first time I had ever been asked. My spirits soared. I signed with a flourish, planting a grateful kiss on their cheeks. As I kissed the young waitress, I felt her stiffen. Looking round I saw the formidable Mrs Armitage striding towards me. Seizing the initiative I took her in my arms and kissed her cheek too. It was clammy and cold to the touch. There was a sharp intake of breath, but before she could respond I was into my bedroom and locking the door. There was a commotion outside, but I didn't hear what was said as I was laughing too much. I felt better. Everything was going to be alright.

* * * * * * * *

My second week at the hotel was a revelation. It was half-term and the hotel was full. The audiences were noisy and appreciative. The weather turned hot. The sun shone down from a cloudless sky. Young schoolgirls, their cheeks reddened by the early summer weather, overcame their intense shyness and formed a ring round my piano, under the watchful eye of their mothers. Captains of industry bought me drinks late into the night. Six- and seven-year-olds were allowed to stay up to watch me as a special treat. During the day I swam and played beach cricket, with their elder brothers. A girl, an attractive blonde of perhaps about 16, became obsessed with me. Although closely chaperoned, I did manage one fevered petting session with her in the woods leading down to the beach.

The pattern of these first two weeks was repeated as I made my way slowly eastwards. Constantine Bay, Lynmouth, Lyme Regis, Torquay. I zigzagged across the coastal area of southern England, sometimes staying only a few days, in others for up to three weeks. My act improved and I gained confidence socially. Money was paid into my bank monthly and yet I had very little to spend it on. Everything was provided: food and lodging, and even my laundry. My only contact with the Goldman organisation was in the form of instructions confirming forthcoming venues. I appeared to be totally on my own. I was never aware of anyone watching my act and reporting back to London.

In August I arrived in Bournemouth. I must have been thoroughly unlikeable. I was living in a false world, shielded from the problems and poverty that gripped most of the country. I learnt to turn on the charm when I thought it would be to my advantage. At other times I could be taciturn, rude and oblivious to other people's feelings. At each venue, some silly young girl would get a 'crush' on me and declare her undying love. I soon learnt that, though the young were ardent, they were too scared of becoming pregnant to satisfy my youthful lust. Gradually I became aware of arch looks from other women. Cards were passed to me, out of the hearing of their husbands. Telephone numbers accumulated and invitations to visit across much of the country. Consequently the young girls were treated by me with the utmost correctness. Parents looked on me as a model of moral rectitude. So it was that my first full sexual experience on tour was with the haughty wife of a leading Cardiff lawyer. Whilst he thrashed around the local links, his wife and I thrashed around their suite at the Grand Hotel in Torquay. In the bed, in the bath and uncomfortably astride the dressing table I was put through my paces. Then, sore and exhausted, I was instructed to make myself scarce as the lawyer would be back shortly. Starting to tidy the mayhem we had inflicted I was told to 'leave it for room service'. I was almost bundled out of the door. I never saw her again. Not that I wanted to. I felt cheapened, aware that I had been used. Every few weeks new opportunities presented themselves. Some were nervous, others racked with guilt. One rather sad woman, in her late thirties, even decided she was in love with me. I think she was unstable. She wrote to me for months. I never replied; by the end of the summer I had lost respect for myself and, in a sense, for women too. These were liaisons without love, just as they had been with the girls in Soho, and – in a way – less honest.

The final week of my tour was at the Metropole on the seafront in Brighton. Many of the clientele had come down from London. They appeared more sophisticated. The ladies' gowns more fashionable, their jewellery more expensive. The men, many smoking cigars, exuded the confidence that only wealth seems to bestow. I judged my opening night to have been a reasonable success. The applause was generous, yet scarcely overwhelming. As usual I drew a number of women to my side, but I thought them rather condescending. From memory, they kept referring to me as cute. I wanted to be sophisticated and vaguely threatening, but to many I remained just a boy.

The following night Harold Goldman arrived with his wife and four guests. They were given a table next to the dance floor. This was to be the first time he had heard me perform in months. Suddenly I was nervous all over again. Had I really improved? Would I meet up to his exacting standards? I feared he might say: "Forget it, Mitch," or, almost as bad, consign me to a secondary provincial tour, playing fleapits and run-down clubs. I wanted to be a star. I needed to be!

That night I gave it everything I had. I was rather alarmed that neither Goldman nor his guests seemed to pay me much attention, just chatting away through most of my numbers. Rather ominously, they all left before I had completed the second half of my act. Goldman just raised a hand in acknowledgement as he rose from the table. I received no follow-up information and, over the rest of the week, I was left agonising as to what the future held for me.

It was strange getting back to the bustle and hubbub of London after a summer spent in the tranquil surroundings of seaside hotels. In Frith Street nothing seemed to have changed, except that Eve had just been released from a month in Holloway for soliciting. Her problem had been as a direct result of investing in a number of new uniforms to supplement her gymslip. The nurse's outfit had been acceptable, but she had gone too far. The magistrate, a devout Catholic, had taken a dim view of her parading the length of Frith Street in a nun's habit, followed by a line of would-be supplicants.

It was strange trying to sleep that night, to the sounds of London traffic and the occasional gasps and groans coming from Eve's apartment. Next morning I slept late, being woken by Antonio informing me I was wanted on the phone. Shocked shoppers looked bemused as, unshaven and wearing only underpants, I took a call from Harold Goldman's secretary. As instructed I presented myself an hour later at his office. He kept me waiting, heightening my nervousness. "Mr Goldman, it's New York for you," the receptionist announced, followed by incoming calls from Paramount and Ivor Novello. I was to learn later that staff put through fictional calls if the lines were slack. The impression had to be of an impresario always busy and in demand. Years later it was sad to see him keeping up this pretence. Like most of us, he was overtaken by younger, even more energetic spirits entering his world.

He took a long time getting to the point that morning, puffing on a thick Havana in the best showbiz tradition. How had my tour gone? Where had I given my best performance? And the worst? My feeling of impending gloom deepened, as he was somewhat critical of my Brighton performance. He informed me he was bringing Fat Man Filkins back over from Paris to tidy up a few sloppy areas, and he had also noticed too much regional intonation in my voice, particularly when speaking. Half an hour into the interview, constantly interrupted by telephone calls, I still didn't really know what the future held. Then he pressed a buzzer on his desk and his secretary came in, clutching a thick, leather-bound folder.

"You'd better sign these." He pushed the open folder to my side of the huge partner's desk. He must have seen the look of doubt cross my face.

"It's alright, your lawyer has been through them. See – here's his initials. He was supposed to witness your signature, but he was too busy this morning and I was not about to argue with him."

I stared stupidly at the contracts, neatly typed on thick cream paper.
"You do read, I take it?" Goldman said. The Café Royal, Chez Victor, Quaglino's. I couldn't take in what I was reading. Harry Goldman came round and embraced me. "Well done, Mitch." I noticed his eyes had filled with tears. "I told you I was going to make you a star. I've had fantastic reports on you, all through the summer". "People are lining up for your signature. This is just a start. In two weeks you open at the Café Royal." His secretary, a lady well into her sixties, kissed me and gave her congratulations. I was numb. They both seemed more excited than me. "There's a lot to do in the next couple of weeks, son." Goldman wiped his eyes with a silk handkerchief, taken from his top pocket. "To start with, you need a haircut. You look like some bloody gypsy." Suddenly all my doubts and reservations evaporated. "I love you," I bawled at the top of my voice, to no one in particular, and the three of us danced an unlikely jig across the thick carpet. The photographs of stars past and present stared down at us. They understood our elation.

* * * * * * * *

Even today, amidst the bustle of Regent Street, it is possible to pass the entrance to the Café Royal without noticing it. Outwardly it has changed little, from the time I made my London debut there. True, it had an illuminated sign above the revolving doors, but the entrance gave no indication as to the size or elegance of the interior. Since the mid-19th century it had been a meeting place for the bohemian set. Sickert and Oscar Wilde held forth there. Rebuilt in 1923, it had lost some of its raffish air, although Augustus John and fellow artists were still to be found regularly in the downstairs luncheon bar.

As my first night approached I had still not been in the building and I was becoming increasingly nervous. Each morning I rehearsed my routine with Fat Man Filkins, in the basement of my Frith Street home. He was a hard taskmaster, but I knew by his reaction to me that I had greatly improved during the summer season. I was also receiving more elocution lessons, and arriving back from one of these sessions at Oxford Circus tube station I decided it was time for me to take a closer look at the Café Royal. Even in those days Regent Street was clogged with traffic. Open-topped double-decker buses fought for position with cars, taxis and the occasional horse-drawn cart. The pavements were crowded with window shoppers and hawkers. Many of the grand stores remain in the same positions today. Liberty, Hamleys, Austin Reed and Aquascutum were already trading successfully. Jays department store held an important site on the corner of Oxford and Regent Street. Galleries Lafayette brought French chic to the east side of the thoroughfare. The large stores were interspersed with small independent shops. A popular meeting place was Stewart's Restaurant, and the *Times* had an office close to the Café Royal.

Rather nervously I slipped into the marble-walled entrance hall. The place was crowded, with a babble of conversation and laughter coming from the bar, whilst elegant couples made their way to the grill room. Moving across to the lift I was taken aback to see my photograph displayed on a metal stand. 'Britain's new singing sensation, Mitch', the notice read, listing the dates of my appearance in the Napoleon room. I took the lift up to the fourth floor. All through my career I have always felt the need to study the layout of the room where I am to perform, no matter how modest. I wanted to make sure the piano was in the best possible position, but also to try and assess the type of atmosphere I was likely to encounter. Away from the crush of the ground floor, the fourth floor appeared deserted. This was a place for night-time entertainment. On a sunny autumn afternoon, it was at rest. I made my way across the Empire room into the much larger Napoleon suite; I peered into a vast chasm, which even the light from the windows behind me failed to pierce. Feeling my way in the darkness I snapped on a batch of light switches. It was a vast room, seemingly the size of a football pitch. Heavy glass fittings hung from an elaborate ceiling. There were five massive doors, each topped by decorative arches. The overall effect was sumptuous. Yellow walls on a bluish background were set off by grand arches in orange, whilst the massive doors glowed a polished brown. The whole room, except for a small dance floor, was carpeted in rich red.

At the far end was the raised bandstand and on it stood a grand piano. Picking my way through the tables, already set for dinner, I mounted the stand and sat on the leather-upholstered stool. I stared out over the army of tables, each with their tiffany lamps, and tried to imagine what I would feel like in a couple of days' time. It was going to be difficult to hold an audience, many of whom were going to be 50 yards away. The kitchens were also alongside the bandstand, behind swing doors; another source of distraction. My thoughts were interrupted by an under-manager, who asked politely if he could help me. I don't know what the poor man thought. I didn't answer him. I simply walked the length of that strange room and down the carpeted staircase into the sunlight, cocooned in my own thoughts.

Harold Goldman allowed me to take a table for four of my chosen guests for my opening night. A stranger quartet it would be hard to imagine. My mother, nervous and quietly appalled by her table companions, wore a new tweed skirt, twin set and pearls. The Fat Man, who was already drunk when he arrived, sported a dinner suit of shimmering blue. I had made Bea and Eve promise to tell mother they were actresses. I wondered if I had been hasty in inviting them, but

they were my best friends in London. Bea looked really quite elegant. She had borrowed a burgundy evening dress, which was topped with somewhat balding fox fur. She had cut down on her make-up and didn't look too out of place. Eve, though, was the show-stopper; I didn't know whether to feel proud of her or just plain embarrassed. Her hair had been shorn, a true short back and sides, parted on the right and slicked down with Brylcreem. She wore flat black shoes, boys' serge trousers, a white shirt, school tie, blazer and make-up. What make-up! A slash of vivid crimson lipstick, false eyelashes and a sea of mascara. She had moved from schoolgirl to provocative schoolboy. Taking off the blazer she was waif thin, but schoolboys don't move like Eve. Several men from surrounding tables jostled to light her cigarette, protruding from the end of a thin, lacquered holder.
I had introduced my mother to her table companions earlier in the evening, explaining that the girls were my flatmates. "What type of roles do you play?" she had asked Eve, after she had recovered somewhat from the Scots girl's appearance. Without a moment's hesitation she replied, "Costume drama, mostly." Bea, smiling, confirmed that her friend specialised in juvenile roles, and the Fat Man reminded us all of her triumphs as a nurse and a policewoman. I was worried things were getting out of control, but I couldn't help joining in the laughter as Eve told my mother that her latest star role had been playing the mother superior of a convent. By this time we were all laughing, uncontrollably, with my poor mother looking at us as if we were quite mad.
Other than that highlight, much of the night is just a blur to me now. I remember it was a difficult audience. I performed against a constant background of conversation. My nervousness soon left me. I concentrated on the tables nearest to me, picking out a number of attractive young girls to direct my lyrics to; polite applause took on some warmth and I was given requests to perform. It was two men who came to the

piano first. They were joined shortly by groups of young girls and a few more mature women. Photographers' bulbs started to flash and the audience seemed reluctant to let me go. In the end my act overran by some 20 minutes. There is always a sense of anticlimax after a performance, when the adrenalin levels are still high. Harold Goldman was on hand to congratulate me. The Fat Man embraced me, informing me that I was: "Shit – but great shit." Somehow I felt Goldman's congratulations were less than fulsome.

I had imagined he would arrange some sort of celebration for me. Perhaps a special dinner, or at least a visit to a club. In fact, I was left with my mother and Bea. Eve had disappeared with a military type, whose companion had apparently been reduced to tears by the Scots girl's tenacity in getting her man. My mother was shocked and disgusted by her behaviour. We dropped her off at her small hotel in Wigmore Street. Getting back into the cab, I gave the driver the address of a small Italian restaurant in Lexington Street that I knew stayed open late. Bea wanted me to drop her off at her flat, insisting there was still time to pull in some punters, but I'm sure she was pleased to be invited to the restaurant.

We sat in the modest trattoria dressed in our evening finery. I hardly said a word. She was like a schoolchild who had been taken on an exciting trip. She chatted about my mother, my performance, the people and the luxury of the Café Royal. I had forgotten that she had already eaten, as she played with the pasta on her plate. I, though, was starving. Eve had apparently been outrageous and the Fat Man increasingly drunk, and yet to Bea it had been a cherished evening. One she assured me she would never forget. We sat long after the last customers had left, drinking fierce red wine and strong coffee. I felt so sorry for Bea. Why didn't she give up this squalid life and go back to the West Country? But I knew better than to raise the subject. Tomorrow she would be back on the streets, the hard-faced hooker. For all her complaints, I

felt in a perverse way she gained some real satisfaction from it.
In the early hours we walked, holding hands, through the largely deserted streets of Soho. It was windy, and fruit wrappers from Berwick Street market whirled and danced about us as we made our way home. "Coming up?" she asked. I hesitated before following her. We lay in her bed, the sweat from our hectic evening still fresh and not unpleasant. Outside the wind had dislodged a dustbin lid, which rattled against the ground with each fresh gust. As I lay there that night, I knew that soon I would be moving on. Leaving for a more fashionable part of town. Bea was already snoring slightly. She lay as I had, as a child, her knees tucked up to her chest. I couldn't sleep. I thought of how many men had shared this bed. I thought of my mother, asleep, anxious to get home to the safety of familiar surroundings; of the Fat Man, lying somewhere in a drunken stupor. And what of Eve? Was this to be the evening when she also moved on, to become a rich man's mistress?
I reached for Bea's hand and squeezed it. Her heavy breathing stopped. I sensed her open her eyes for a second, then her hand tightened on mine. "You were great tonight, Mitch," she mumbled. "You are going to be a star and you'll forget me – all of us," she added as an afterthought.
I protested. "I'll never forget any of you, whatever happens."
But, of course, I did.

CHAPTER 15

Within weeks of my London debut I moved to a small but comfortable apartment in Seymour Place. It had the advantage of being in a modern block, was central and yet not too expensive. I didn't exactly slink away from Frith Street, but I moved my few possessions quickly and this time there were no fond farewells. Soho had served its purpose. I was moving on to a different lifestyle.

Over the next few years I would see some of the girls I used to know, standing on street corners as I visited one of the fashionable restaurants in the area. If noticed, I would raise my hand in lofty recognition, but I made it a rule to never speak to them. I possibly felt a passing guilt, but I was too self-obsessed to look back. Luckily, Bea seemed to disappear from the scene. I did hear a rumour that she had been slashed by a pimp. I chose to think that she had heeded my warning and gone back to a life of respectability in Bristol. Strangely, it was Eve that I saw constantly. She had indeed moved upmarket. For years she appeared, in increasingly outrageous outfits, on Curzon Street, in the heart of Mayfair. Sadly, in her profession, time at the top is limited. It was well after the end of the war, as I was travelling by taxi to Paddington station, that I saw a raddled yet recognisable figure, standing under a lamp-post, in Praed Street. I paid my cabby off and went over to her. Close to, she looked quite frightening – a parody of the young girl I had met over 20 years before. Her face was caked in powder, her eyes dilated and her lipstick smeared over her mouth, as if it had been applied in the dark.

"Eve, it's Mitch." She didn't appear to hear me. I was overwhelmed by a smell of drink, sweat and sickly sweet, cheap perfume. "Quid for a quickie, darling," she lisped. She showed no sign of recognising me. I pushed a crisp white fiver into her hand. "Och, it's the works you want?" I tried to explain I didn't want anything from her. At first she looked shocked, then annoyed. "Fucking pervert," she shouted at my retreating back. I should have realised – a woman scorned and all that! As usual, any kindness I revealed tended to rebound on me.

My launch onto the London scene was relatively well reviewed in the musical press. Similarly, audiences were polite rather than enthusiastic. Some nights went really well, others were horribly flat. Performing cabaret requires very particular skills. I still had some learning to do. My playing was second to none and my voice developing, but as yet not distinctive enough. It needed to be instantly recognisable. The main problem, though, was my lack of reaction to each specific audience. I needed to develop some off-the-cuff repartee. Many famous stage performances have bombed, attempting to engage a rowdy cabaret gathering.

By the New Year it was obvious that, contrary to Harry Goldman's predictions, I was not about to become an overnight star. My bookings were moved to secondary venues, but luckily this worked in my favour. The NOT club was a well-known proving ground for developing talent. It was situated in a small basement, below the Café Anglaise, in Leicester Square. The place was little more than a speakeasy, with tables crammed together and guests perched on flimsy chairs. This was where the rich and well connected liked to think they were slumming it. Goldman signed me on for a lengthy season, just prior to the club being extended into the already flourishing Café Anglaise.

The intimate atmosphere suited me and I found I was able to hold and involve the audiences. Now the *New Musical Express* informed their readers of a blossoming talent, whilst *Melody Maker* stated that my act rivalled any of the established stars. My confidence grew. I started my performance at 11:00, as the diners tucked into the house speciality of kippers and beer. The fact that the club was so informal and didn't require evening dress appealed to its well-connected clientele. I was singing for and being cheeky to the aristocracy and the stars of the theatre, who tended to troop in after their shows had finished. Gertrude Lawrence, Gloria Swanson and Clifford Webb all turned up one night. I was introduced to leading names featured in Debrett's – the Milford Havens, Brecknocks and Carnarvons. Woolworth heiress Barbara Hutton even appeared with her latest husband.

I didn't know where the recommendation came from, but one morning nearing the end of my run at the NOT I received a phone call from Martin Poulsen, the Danish owner of the Café de Paris. He informed me that the Prince of Wales had requested me to appear at Poulsen's restaurant. This was quite the most prestigious venue in London. I was overjoyed; I knew this was the breakthrough I had been waiting for. At that time it was reckoned that a hard core, of perhaps some 3,000 people, kept the fashionable clubs and restaurants of London afloat. These were made up largely of aristocrats who had inherited money through the generations and still never had to work. They were supplemented by a new breed of super-rich, self-made men. At the head of both these groups was the Prince of Wales. Where he led the others followed. The Café de Paris was constantly packed, as it was known that the royal party visited the place regularly, often several times in a week, if the cabaret was to his liking. It was only his patronage, in the early days of its existence, that had allowed the restaurant to survive. Coventry Street had previously been better known for its pimps and prostitutes. Gradually, though, the oval, two-tiered basement acquired the reputation as the place to be seen.

Approached through double glass doors, the decor was an exact replica of the palm court aboard the doomed liner *Lusitania*. Entering the bridge there was a central lobby with a view of the whole restaurant. Twin staircases, each of 21 steps, swooped down to the dance floor. Diners instinctively looked up to view every entrance, as gentlemen in tailed suits escorted their ladies to their allotted tables. Formal dress was essential to gain entry to the dance area. The balcony was reserved for lesser mortals and those who chose to wear dinner jackets. The table immediately adjoining the dance floor, at the bottom of the right-hand staircase, was permanently reserved for His Royal Highness. The resident band, that of Jack Harris, was housed in a recess under the bridge. I always insisted that the piano was brought out onto the edge of the dance floor for my performance. The Café de Paris had an atmosphere that was unique, and it was only after the early sitting, when the provincial set had left, that the place came into its own.

I had hardly started playing on my first night there before the royal party arrived. The prince didn't even sit down. He led his partner onto the floor, as I sang *Time on my hands*. I had been warned that I had to continue playing non-stop until His Royal Highness sat down. Half an hour later, as I moved into *Blue moon*, the prince still swayed on the crowded dance floor, watched surreptitiously by most, but certainly not approached. At last he sat down, to loud applause. For him, of course, rather than me.

At the end of the evening I was called over to the royal table and congratulated. Camera bulbs flashed. I reminded the prince of our previous meeting, at my village school. He thought for a moment, his face lighting up. "I remember, quite the little urchin." Everyone laughed; sycophancy ruled supreme then, but I was made. The later editions of the dailies had photographs recording our meeting. 'Mitch the urchin' proclaimed the *Express*. Predictably, the *Mail* recorded 'A new star is born'. Overnight I was a big name. The prince came to see me on five more occasions, during my two-week run. I was offered recording contracts by Decca and Parlophone, and I appeared on the BBC for the first time.

Harry Goldman was not happy, however. The booking at the Café de Paris had been made without any reference to him.

How could I be so disloyal? I had made him look a fool. And the papers; "What a disaster," he declared. Here he was, trying to build a mysterious background for me. The son of an unnamed nobleman, educated abroad. Now I had admitted to being "some bloody country bumpkin," he fumed. And where had I got my poncey accent from? He was beside himself. "There's too much bloody truth around," he concluded. "Don't you understand that the punters want a little magic in their lives?"
In fact, over the coming weeks there was extensive coverage of me, with interviews with my mother and Theddington villagers. The story of 'country boy shop assistant made good' won me a far wider audience. I moved effortlessly towards stardom. I was making huge money, up to £300 a week. This was soon to double. I was good-looking in a rather coarse way, urbane, and able to mix in any company. I dressed lavishly and was seen at all the right social events. I rode in Rotten Row, attended Royal Ascot and hunted periodically with the Quorn. I frequented boxing matches, Wimbledon and Henley. I joined the Eccentric Club in Jermyn Street, much favoured by the acting profession. More establishment clubs proved harder to breach.
I was hot property. Over the next couple of years I played all the leading London and provincial venues. I extended my work to theatres, even surviving the Glasgow Empire, but this was really not my scene. I never enjoyed being backed by large bands; they took away from the intimacy of my act. Eventually I did make it to be top of the bill at the Palladium. But, although I had good reviews, I didn't enjoy the experience. I made my New York debut in the Starlight room at the Waldorf Astoria, on the first part of a world tour. This was considered to be a vital test, but the Yanks loved me and my material. I moved on to Hong Kong, Singapore, Kuala Lumpur and Mombasa. Each summer I moved out of town, to perform in Nice, Monte Carlo and Deauville. It was there that

my interest in racing started. I bought two thoroughbred fillies and sent them to a leading trainer in Newmarket. I started gambling. It was a period when thoroughbred fillies of the two-legged variety also featured strongly in my life. I was seen with the daughters of many leading aristocratic dynasties on my arm. Well-known actresses also featured strongly. Married women, silly young girls – all came and went. It was a false world. One where everyone seemed to dedicate themselves to excess and pleasure; and yet, the harder it was sought, the more elusive it became. I smoked, drank, gambled, performed to increasing acclaim, and made love. No, that's wrong; I had sex. Emotions, other than at the most superficial level, were considered dangerous. Love was bandied about in public. "I just love your playing, darling – too divine!" "He's the love of my life, I swear!" All this was fine for public consumption, but in the confines of the bedroom emotions were rarely mentioned; love, never. Bad form, you know!

My day would start with me rising to take a light luncheon at my club or Scott's. Afternoons were spent at the races, or with a tea dance, at the Ritz or Claridges. Then I tended to take an early evening nap, followed by drinks prior to my performance. After my act, I would move on to a club for more cocktails. Then it was back to my flat, to tumble drunkenly into bed, with whoever happened to be involved with me at the time. These affairs tended to be short-lived, due, no doubt, to my increasing boorishness.

Amongst vague memories of thrashing limbs, one candidate stands out. A minor member of foreign royalty. A lady much older than myself, she insisted on making love whilst wearing a tiara and enough jewellery to stock Tiffany's. Very exciting at first, but ultimately extremely uncomfortable.

The more outwardly successful my life became, a terrible feeling of emptiness and of being strangely unfulfilled developed within me. My attention span was fitful. I spent even more lavishly, in an attempt to erase the feelings of doubt. Newly acquired interests bored me, as quickly as my constantly changing girlfriends. Both Ivor Novello and Noel Coward tried to convince me that young men would be the answer to my malaise. It was only with the greatest difficulty, in a suite at the Savoy, that I managed finally to convince Noel that this was *not* the answer for me.

I sold the racehorses and bought a succession of powerful sports cars. I tried racing at Brooklands. I wrote the vehicle off on the second corner, and spent ten days in hospital. I was becoming hyperactive, always looking for something new to distract me. I tried cocaine. Luckily, it made me sick. Harry Goldman was becoming concerned. I was charged with being drunk and disorderly outside the Savoy. Over this period I was arrested on at least three other occasions. Each time the charges were dropped There were powerful forces working on my behalf. Money was deducted from earnings, under the heading 'legal expenses'. Illegal, more like!

It was in the middle of this period, when I was beginning to spin out of control, that I received a call from my mother. I had probably been in London for about three years and yet I had never gone home to see her. Guilt even managed to penetrate my self-obsession. I was still just sensitive enough to realise that I had turned into the type of person that even I would have despised earlier in my life. She rang to tell me that Lettice Champion had broken her back in a hunting accident. It was the tone of the voice, rather than what she said, that implied criticism. The Champions had come too see me once at Romano's but, looking back, I had to acknowledge that, on that night, I had acted as if I was, in some way, conferring an honour on them by highlighting their existence to the other diners. In fact, it was to them that I owned much of my success. I heard myself tell my mother that I would be up to see her the following day. I assume I had a gap in my

engagements. I can't imagine I was unselfish enough to cancel an earning opportunity.
I hired a chauffeur to drive me in my Daimler to Theddington. Champion House seemed smaller; I had become accustomed to staying at stately piles. Smaller, maybe, but still stylish. That night I felt uncomfortable as I ate alone, in the grand dining room. I was told that Mrs Champion was too tired to see me until the morning. I was rather miffed. Mr Champion was away on business. I invited my mother to join me, but was told this would not be correct. She seemed wary of me. She retained the ability she had when I was young, of looking at me and seeming to be able to tell what I had done wrong. It was rather unnerving. How had I become so detached from her, when once she had been the most important person in my life? I had taken her in my arms on my arrival, but she stayed passive as I kissed her. She looked at me without any joy, assessing me in my fine clothes and not liking what she saw. I was aware of other staff in the background, the young maids open-mouthed at seeing me close up at last. I had brought presents for my mother, gift-wrapped from Harvey Nichols. She placed the large boxes on a table before showing me to my room. She was the housekeeper, not my mother. I hated the atmosphere she was creating. I wanted her to proudly introduce me to all the staff, so I could be charming and bask in their adulation and my own self-importance.
"Mum!" I implored. "What's the matter? You seem so different." She looked at me for what seemed an eternity. "Oh, Bob," she whispered; "it's not me that's changed," and she scurried from the room.
Lettice Champion had certainly not changed. At least, not from the waist up, and that is all I saw of her as she lay in a huge bed propped up by soft down pillows. "The prodigal returns," she said, holding her hands out in welcome. "Here, let me look at you." She had wonderful green eyes, and they seemed to search my soul. I had brought her a present from

Liberty's. "I remembered it was your favourite store," I said. She pulled at the ribbon. "That was thoughtful of you, Bob." She had retained the Irish lilt to her voice, and although she smiled the tone was almost one of rebuke. "Do you normally buy old, crippled ladies nightdresses?" she asked, holding the sheer negligée up to the light. "Or is it one of your girlfriends' rejects?"

"I chose it myself; I thought it would suit your colouring." I was hurt and annoyed.

"Now, don't go getting on your high horse. Sit down, Bob. I'm sorry; it's beautiful."

The atmosphere relaxed and she told me about the accident. She did not intend to become bedridden and I believed her when she said, that with the help of the latest wheelchair, she would soon be mobile again. We chatted on, but I sensed that there was something on her mind and she was waiting for an opportunity to raise it. This became apparent after my mother had departed, having brought in coffee and biscuits. Lettice Champion started falteringly, by telling me that my mother had become her great friend. Because of this she felt obliged to tell me how unhappy I had made her. I tried to agree, to deflect her, but she was in full flow now, eyes flashing, colour heightened. How could I treat my mother so? She had wanted to be proud of me. She silenced my protests. In fact, Connie was ashamed of me. I had ignored her and all my oldest friends. My scandalous behaviour was common knowledge. How could I show such insensitivity and be so arrogant? I tried to explain that I lived in a different world now, but she would have none of it.

"You've found fame but lost your way." She started sobbing. I felt confused. Was this what my mother really felt, or was it an excuse for a recently crippled woman to let off steam? "Take stock now, boy, before it's too late." I thought she was being melodramatic. I was a good guy – everyone loved me.

Any pity I had for the woman evaporated. How dare she spout all that rubbish.
I went back to my room. The sooner I left this claustrophobic atmosphere the better. People were expecting too much of me. I went downstairs in search of the chauffeur. In the hall I found my mother. She looked as if she had been crying. God, I thought; this place is a bloody madhouse.
I told my mother about Mrs Champion's reaction to me. "She shouldn't have spoken to you like that. It wasn't her place." I pompously agreed. "The accident. It's terrible, it's just too much for such an active woman."
"I forgive her," I said opening the door to the staff quarters, hoping to spot the wretched chauffeur. It was the look my mother gave that stopped me in my tracks. It didn't indicate hatred, just abject despair. Her shoulders heaved as she tried to hold back the tears. She looked old and vulnerable, and yet I was reminded of that young mother who sat with me each night, brushing her hair. I had loved her so much then. I suppose I still loved her, but it was an emotion that had great trouble entering my consciousness now. I took her in my arms. I felt upset.
"Don't ruin your life, Bob." I assured her I would be fine. God, let me get out of here, I thought. Then, almost as an afterthought, she informed me that Kitty had been home for a couple of days and had hoped to see me.
I pushed her away from me. "What, do you mean to tell me Kitty has been home all the time whilst I've been hanging around here?"
"I thought you came to see Mrs Champion?" she said.
"Damn Mrs Champion. What time does she leave?"
"She's going back to Scotland. She's catching the 3:30 from Stratton."
Outside a winter fog had descended. I drove like a lunatic down to the station. Luckily there was hardly any traffic on the road. Several times I lost my bearings altogether,

mounting muddy verges and scraping the paintwork against leafless branches. I screeched into the forecourt and, leaving the engine running, sprinted past the objecting ticket collector. It was already past 3:30 and I cursed as, peering through the mist, the platform appeared to be deserted. Either I had missed her or Kitty had gone to Peterborough, to catch the train that went through to Edinburgh without the need to change. Seething, I was just about to leave when I thought I heard a distant train approaching. Through the gloom, I could just make out some figures appearing from the waiting room. I charged down the platform.
"Kitty!" I shouted her name so loudly that everyone turned to watch this demented figure running towards them. She looked slightly ridiculous. She was wearing a long, shapeless coat, a college scarf, and a knitted beret worn at a jaunty angle. It was very dark and murky, but I could see the look of surprise on her face. She was already boarding the train.
"Must you go? Can't you get a later train?"
"I can't, I'll miss my connection; anyway, I'm on duty in the morning." I offered to drive her to Peterborough, but there wasn't time. She undid the leather strap and lowered the window. A porter was loading some parcels from a trolley into the guard's carriage. I held her hand.
"You're a doctor," I said.
"Not yet I'm not. Finals next year. You're the success. I never thought I'd ever know anyone famous." A whistle sounded. I could feel her breath on my face. Her hands were icy cold. The train started to move, puffing, snorting as it built up steam. I was conscious of specks of soot settling on my face. Staring into her dark eyes I felt a strange emptiness in my stomach. She really didn't look that pleased to see me.
"I haven't changed," I blurted out as I started to trot alongside the moving carriage. For the first time a huge smile lit up her face. "Not much! Write to me, you lazy devil."

I was running now, still grabbing at her hand. "Come and see me in London," I shouted. I didn't hear her reply. As I walked slowly back down the platform, I felt something drop from my coat. Bending, I picked up a bracelet that must have become dislodged from her wrist. It was one that Kitty had worn since that first day I met her. Back in the car I switched on the light. It was a child's bangle, with strange Eastern charms hanging from it. I remember holding it to my cheek before tenderly kissing the cold metal. Tears streamed down my face, and even then I didn't know why.

CHAPTER 16

The supper delivered by room service is disgusting. The sauce has been absorbed by the pasta and forms a glutinous mass. The side salad must have been lying about for hours. Limp lettuce leaves, with an overripe tomato, overwhelmed by pungent onion and a sickly dressing. I wish I had left it all untouched. Now my stomach rumbles ominously and I have a dull pain in my chest. I'm looking forward to getting home to Maria. No, that's nonsense! At my age, you don't look forward – just back, churning over your life. Why am I so miserable, for God's sake? I have generally enjoyed good health, travelled extensively and plied whatever talent I had, to great effect. I have experienced huge wealth and an admiring public. And yet? I know the missing component is love, both given and received. Now, as I lie here, I am racked by guilt, regret and fear. Guilt, about the way I treated one person I did love, my mother; also, at the cavalier manner I used friends when they were in a position to be of help to me, only to drop them later. Regret, that I wasted so much of my life on a sea of booze, insincerity and self-obsession. The fear is harder to define: it's been with me since I was a child, given oxygen by Kitty's unexplained death, and is with me still.

I was tempted to keep Kitty's bracelet as a good luck charm. For a time we wrote to each other, every few days, but gradually I was drawn back by the excitement and glamour to my old ways. Soon I was getting my secretary to compose and type my letters to Kitty, leaving me just to sign them with a flourish. Since moving into a sizeable apartment in Basil Street I had acquired quite a retinue of staff, including a butler. My career continued to blossom and I surrounded myself with dubious companions. They were welcome, as long as they fed my insatiable ego with constant compliments. In a temperamental outburst I refused to renew my recording contract with Parlophone, and defected to HMV for a marginally greater percentage. In fact Parlophone had done an amazing job in producing staggering sales for my records, but I didn't think I owed anyone my loyalty. I was convinced that commercial organisations, as well as lovers, had to come to me on my terms.

Then came a real setback. Signed to make three films, the first, *From Paris with love*, was a disaster. So bad, in fact, that the other two were never made. I sang just one number in the movie, which was essentially a drama. The script was terrible, the plot weak, and I was hopelessly wooden. My speaking voice came across as if I had been grabbed round the windpipe. The critics tore the film to shreds and my performance was rightly ridiculed. It was a financial disaster for the studio, never even being offered for general release. Twenty years later I again failed in early television productions. I needed the intimacy of a club or a restaurant. Cameras do strange things to people. As a true artist I was better seen in the flesh, I concluded.

Eventually Kitty's letters became more intermittent. Janet, my secretary, would read them to me as I lay in bed taking a late breakfast. I was receiving a huge amount of fan mail, all of which was answered by one of three standard letters. Autograph requests were particularly irksome and tended to be signed either by Janet or my butler. Ignore your fans at your peril! I did arrange for flowers to be sent to Kitty, on news of her becoming qualified. I even wrote the card.

By now I was at the height of my fame. I acquired my own white grand piano, which was transported to whichever British venue I was appearing at. I declined invitations to all but the grandest houses. Looking back, I was a snob, name-dropper and buffoon. Not a serious thought entered my head. My massive earnings, wisely invested, would have ensured considerable comfort for the rest of my life. Instead I haemorrhaged money. I never bought a property in London, moving to a succession of increasingly expensive and prestigious apartments. For a time, I even kept a permanent suite at the Savoy. My mother had always urged that 'everything in moderation' was the way to achieve happiness. I tried the opposite route. Overeating, binge drinking and indiscriminate sex sessions. Gradually, this way of living dulls the senses. Nothing excites. You find yourself wanting a simple meal, or a refreshing lime juice, instead of a gin fizz. During these brief periods of abstinence, I even abandoned the comfort of my huge bed for a single divan in the spare room. It was a refuge for me, lying there cocooned in fresh sheets and warm blankets. A relief not to be obliged to go through increasingly irritating overtures, with women who tended to be forgotten in days. Lying in that small divan, I was reminded of my childhood and the sense of security I felt then. My new period of denial was noted and commented on. In fact, I was sliding into an even worse phase; I now drank alone. Destructive drinking, which had to be assuaged on waking. I stopped early in the evening, slept and was able to give passable performances. I no longer hung around the clubs, but took a cab home to resume a solitary session into the early hours. Perhaps twice a week I took a trip to Shepherds Market. No tedious preliminaries here. No promises to be made, only to be broken the next day. Here the girls understood the arrangement. Whilst I fell into a drunken stupor they would take their fee from my wallet. I was always welcome.

Then I met Tilly Nash. Her father had started life as a shoddy dealer, but was now one of the country's leading knitting wool spinners. Tilly had been privately educated and sent to a finishing school in Switzerland. A slim, angelic-looking blonde, she had retained her native Yorkshire common sense. Her well-modulated voice could lurch into that of a Bradford mill girl, with matching vocabulary if annoyed. For several months she was to exert considerable influence over me and I still look back on her with real affection.

Nightclubs were really not Tilly's scene, although once we had met she did tend to follow me round, making sure I behaved myself. I don't think she was jealous, just possessive. We met at a smart cocktail party, given by a Tory MP who had a flat overlooking Horse Guards Parade. Tilly had only recently arrived in London, with a view – I subsequently decided – to finding a suitable husband. She had the bluest of innocent eyes and the cutest upturned nose. Only her rather square-set jaw gave any indication of the formidable personality that lay behind her childlike features.
I drank lemon cordial that day, but my face and breath told any inquisitive onlooker another story. I had a frightful headache and, generally bored with the company, I was stealthily making my way to the front door when she introduced herself. She had recognised me and knew of my reputation. From that first meeting, she set out to change me and the way I lived. At first I assumed she would just be another easy conquest. I was so wrong.
"You can keep your hands to yourself, until you've seen a good pox doctor," she informed me. "I've heard all about your shenanigans." Amazingly, I found myself obeying her instructions. Just as well, as it happens! In a matter of weeks she had taken over my life. My drinking and womanising she could forgive. Many men, given the chance, were guilty of these, but what really appalled her was my attitude to money. She turned my dining room into an office and pored over receipts and unopened bank statements. I came back one afternoon to discover she had fired Rowney, my butler, on the spot for falsifying the household accounts. He didn't argue, and neither did I. You didn't argue with Tilly. I just enjoyed being swept along by her.
Although I was earning a fortune, I had virtually no savings. What money I had resided in current accounts. Her father's stockbroker was summoned and an accountant appointed. She put a ban on new clothes for me. Money was to be invested

each month on a regular basis. "Why rent property?" she demanded, and leading estate agents were briefed.
She was horrified by my indolence. "You'll be a butterball by the time you're 40," she insisted. I was introduced to tennis and golf, both of which she played with gusto. I couldn't get to grips with golf. I needed something more instantaneous. We went to the Queen's Club each morning, for a couple of sets before lunch. We spent all our waking hours together, with Tilly escorting me home straight after my last performance. Sometimes we stayed in her mews house off Bryanston Square, but it was always to separate bedrooms that we went, after a modest nightcap together. There was no way I was going to have my wicked way; not completely, anyway. It was a strangely comforting period of my life. I didn't have to think. It was like having a personal assistant, who attended to all my needs.
We travelled up to Yorkshire to meet her family. Her father viewed me with some suspicion. He disliked most southerners, and crooners, he felt, were as much use as a eunuch in a whorehouse. Mrs Nash, I could tell, thought differently. "Take no notice of Ted," she insisted; "he's a philistine." I realised that Tilly and her mother had marriage in mind. I was almost swept along by the idea. My whole life had changed. My financial affairs were showing a massive improvement. Early morning runs and tennis had brought a healthy glow to my face. Waistbands to trousers had to be taken in.
Tilly began to hint that it was time we were engaged. I tried to deflect her, but it was difficult. "Do you want me to pop the question?" she finally demanded. I made excuses. I needed to find a suitable house; I had an overseas tour being negotiated. I was fond of Tilly, but in truth I was becoming bored. I longed for just one night on the town. She was always at my side. It was claustrophobic. I had also been celibate for six months. I was missing the excitement of

seduction, being drunk, rowdy and irresponsible. It was whilst I was grappling with this dilemma that, unexpectedly, I received a telephone call from Kitty. She had apparently recently taken up a post at Shenley, a mental hospital in Hertfordshire. In those days they were referred to as 'lunatic asylums'. I asked her to meet me in London, but she was working shifts that didn't end till 10:00 at night and she had no transport. The following Thursday was to be my final night's appearance after a fortnight's run at the Café de Paris.
"Why don't I send my chauffeur to pick you up after work? You'll still be in time for the second part of my act."
"Chauffeur, indeed," she giggled, but she still seemed doubtful. "I've got nothing to wear; I was a student until a few months ago, you know."
Loftily I assured her that whatever she wore would be fine; "And don't worry about accommodation, I'll book you into a hotel."
"Golly," she said; "are you sure? Actually, I have a day's holiday due, so I could spend Friday exploring London."
Tilly was not overjoyed by the news. She was aware of Kitty, because she read all my correspondence. Kitty's letter were always similar, chatty and confining herself to telling me about her work or occasional trips into the Scottish countryside. There was never an inkling of any romance, other than the way she signed off each letter with 'my love to you, as always'. Tilly became noticeably more irritable as my final night at the Café de Paris approached. Perhaps she, rather than I, sensed the significance of the meeting with Kitty. She was quite intuitive as well as being a very forceful personality.
It's hard for me to remember my emotions at the prospect of meeting Kitty again. For all I knew she could have been married. She had never mentioned any romantic attachments, but no attractive woman is without a string of admirers.

Tilly wanted to know where Kitty would be staying. "We have no room here and I don't want a stranger in my house, thank you." Her manner was quite aggressive, so I didn't tell her that the Ritz had been fully booked except for one luxury suite and that I had reserved it for Kitty. Just the thrill of booking this extravagance appealed to me. Tilly's baby blue eyes seemed to bore in on me as I lied and told her I had booked a modest hotel off the Edgware Road.

The previous week I had been summoned to Tilly's father's London club and told in no uncertain manner that people were talking about us and matters had to be regularised. I pretended I didn't understand. Nash spluttered, "Damn it, you soft booger, it's time the two of you got engaged." I tried to tell him I wasn't good enough for his daughter. He didn't disagree, but I had been given the most direct of signals. I was trapped.

These disconcerting thoughts were uppermost in my mind, rather than Kitty's arrival, as I started my performance that evening. They were a receptive audience and soon my troubles retreated as the applause grew. I never tired of applause. The adrenalin increased and I basked in its warmth. I had drunk two Martini cocktails in my dressing room prior to going on. It was an act of defiance. Under the new regime, Tilly insisted I didn't drink until I was home. I performed better when I was slightly tipsy. I was relaxed, my voice soft as velvet, my hands caressing the keys and my repartee razor-sharp.

I felt Tilly's hand tense on my shoulder. I noticed people at the tables closest to me were staring up towards the bridge. Every entry into the restaurant tended to be theatrical. It had been designed to create a sense of drama. The tension transmitted by Tilly and a faint collective intake of breath caused me to look up.

"Oh my God, she's a black!" Tilly hissed. I ignored her. Forgetting the audience I stopped playing. Slowly I rose from my stool. I met her halfway up the staircase. She looked embarrassed, but she smiled nervously. I took her arm and escorted her to a table that still had Tilly's evening bag on it. The room was completely quiet and I remember the rustle of Kitty's sari and the coolness of her skin. We still hadn't spoken, and returning to the piano I apologised to my audience and introduced Kitty as my oldest childhood friend. "Sweetheart?" a bejewelled dowager enquired, and everyone in the room except Tilly seemed to be laughing.

Without any forethought I started singing *Zing went the strings of my heart*; the audience broke into spontaneous applause. Kitty looked confused, Tilly furious, and I felt a surge of elation the like of which I had never experienced. Tilly sat with her back half turned to Kitty, whilst I played six or seven other numbers. I was on top form. I showed off, I flirted, and I led some raucous community singing with a group of young people who insisted that Kitty join them as they surrounded the piano. The audience wouldn't let me go.

Tilly left before the end. She must have sensed that we were finished. We continued seeing each other for a few weeks, but it was time to move on.

We parted good friends, with her warning me not to go back to my old ways. She never married, although her restless energy saw her become one of Britain's foremost businesswomen. She sold the family mills before the decline in knitting and invested heavily in property. By the time of her death she had become fabulously wealthy, and had set up a number of influential charitable trusts.

I had booked Kitty's suite for two nights, so that we could have a whole day together seeing the sights. She was overwhelmed and embarrassed by the opulence of the Ritz. "You're mad," she said as she moved from the large, richly carpeted sitting room into the panelled bathroom; "how much does this cost?" I smiled, enjoying her childlike excitement. Every nook had to be explored. She ran the bath, threw open the cocktail cabinet and drew the heavy brocade curtains to look down on a deserted Piccadilly. I opened a bottle of champagne and she giggled as the froth bubbled over onto the carpet. "To us!" I said. She averted my gaze and seemed serious for a moment. "To you, Mitch. You were tremendous; I'm so sorry I interrupted your performance. I could have died walking down those stairs." I told her how proud I was; it was an entrance fit for a queen. I took her hand, but she broke away.

"Why did your girlfriend leave? I get the impression she doesn't approve of me."

"I do, though," I said, raising my glass, but again she shyly looked away. We talked well into the night. There was a lot of catching up to do. Gradually, as if unwrapping a valuable present, we discovered what had happened to us since we last met. We talked about our work, our friends, but avoiding any mention of romantic attachments. Then we were back to the childhood memories. We laughed and joked, and yet I was shocked by my attraction to her. I was captivated, feeling strangely disorientated. Eventually she declared that she was exhausted. For a moment, I though she was going to invite me to stay. Instead she went slowly to the entrance and held the door open for me. I felt astonishingly nervous and inadequate. I wanted to sweep her into my arms. Instead, awkwardly, I shook her hand and thanked her for coming to see me. My throat was dry, but I did manage to tell her I thought she looked sensational. Now it was her turn to appear uncertain. She gabbled something to the effect that's she hoped wearing a sari hadn't embarrassed me. "I'm afraid I can't afford evening dresses yet," she said. She was talking very quickly and not making much sense. Tentatively I placed my hands on her shoulders. "Oh, Kitty," was all I could say.

"I don't think I should have come," she whispered. There were tears in her eyes. Darting forward, she tenderly kissed my cheek, before gently closing the door.

* * * * * * * *

I didn't go home that night, frightened I might be confronted by Tilly. I found an all-night café and munched on a bacon sandwich, alongside workmen on night shift. I did manage to snatch a couple of hours' sleep before, showered and shaved, I presented myself back at Ritz. I can't really remember what we did that morning. I have no recollection of us eating lunch, but I do know that, after much persuasion, I bought Kitty an amazing outfit for our evening meal at Quaglino's. We staggered into the hotel foyer loaded with boxes and took the lift to the top floor. I remember throwing open the windows. There was a small balcony outside and, above it, a parapet. I still stop and stare upwards when I pass the Ritz. How could we have taken such a risk? Somehow I had clambered up and hauled Kitty after me. Love does strange things to you. Kitty held onto my arm as, legs dangling, we looked down on the clogged traffic and the scurrying pedestrians, the size of mice. Showing off I staggered to my feet and, swaying in a stiff breeze, pretended to be Mussolini, addressing a vast crowd in Rome. Kitty implored me to get down. Petrified, she slipped slowly onto the balcony. Not to be outdone, I jumped from the parapet, landing awkwardly. A shaft of pain ran through my ankle as it turned on landing. Losing my balance I fell into her arms. With the roar of the traffic below as a background, I kissed her. This time she didn't resist.

What else do I remember that day? Certainly the yellow gown I had brought her, and her plaited hair. The effect she had on people, of which she seemed totally unaware.

That night we became lovers. It was largely at her instigation. I really wanted to preserve the moment, for when we were married. Old-fashioned, perhaps, but true. For marriage was where I was convinced we were destined. Our lovemaking seemed strangely unreal. I still remember the smoothness of her skin and the musky fragrance of her perfume. There was a charged tenderness, but little passion. No word was spoken, the spell not breached. We slept like children that night, in each other's arms.

In the morning Kitty was embarrassed and awkward. We never made love again. It was never discussed. Years later, I began to doubt if it had really happened.

Our working schedules made it difficult for us to meet more than once a week. I used to motor out to Shenley, to pick her up at the forbidding entrance to the collection of ugly red-bricked buildings. Sometimes she came to stay with me in London. By now, we were totally at ease in each other's company. I never tried to force myself on her and she usually slept in the spare room. We discussed our future together. She was worried that our lifestyles were incompatible. She was dedicated to her future in medicine, although she was having second thoughts about staying in mental welfare. Marriage was discussed, and I regret I never formally asked her. Somehow I just assumed that this was the likely outcome. The nearest we came to a formal engagement was one day when, standing outside Garrards, I insisted on buying her a ring. I think I was still frightened of being rejected, and certainly she declined looking at any of the displays of formal jewellery. Instead she led me through to a smaller showroom, at the rear of the shop that dealt in second-hand and antique jewellery. A frock-coated salesman offered tray after tray of cameo brooches and Victorian pendants. We had been through almost the entire stock before Kitty lifted a ring and said without hesitation, "This one, please."

The ring was an ancient Egyptian scarab. The gold band looked to have been made for a man, and it fitted her forefinger perfectly. Outside, on a sunny Regent Street, I asked her if the ring meant we were engaged. She smiled. "It means I love you, Mitch; always."
During the summer Kitty changed. Not in her attitude to me – she was still attentive and loving – but she appeared to have something on her mind that she was not sharing with me. She was nervous and generally unhappy. It appeared she was experiencing difficulty with one particular patient. He was a schizophrenic, who had become fixated with Kitty. He didn't threaten her but insisted that he knew her from a previous life. I though it strange that she was upset by such nonsense. He would follow her obsessively down the dark corridors of the hospital and turn up at her office without warning. She felt he was watching her all the time. I caught sight of him one time when I went to pick Kitty up from reception at Shenley. "Who's that?" I asked her, indicating a retreating figure dressed in black as he ducked behind a privet hedge. "That's him – my problem," she said.
"You didn't tell me he was a priest."
"He isn't; he just insists on dressing like one." I didn't pursue the subject, but a couple of weeks later Kitty surprised me by announcing she was going back to Stratton Market to take up general practice. She maintained that we would be able to see more of each other. I was due to go off on a tour to France in the autumn, and she said that, providing we both felt the same about each other, perhaps that would be the time to consider marriage. I was overjoyed; I told her to go house-hunting in my absence. The thought of dividing time between London and the country suddenly had an overwhelming appeal.
Kitty was safely employed as Dr Bell's assistant in Stratton Market when, a couple of months later, I left for France. With Shenley behind her she was quite her old self again. I

couldn't wait for my tour to be completed, so that we could officially announce our engagement.
I opened at the Westminster Hotel in Le Touquet, and after a week I moved on to Deauville. With war threatening, there was some talk as to whether I should travel on down to Nice. There was an expensive penalty clause that could be invoked if I failed to turn up, and Harry Goldman insisted I must honour my contract.
I rose late on Sunday, September the 3rd. The previous evening had been a great success, particularly as I had performed several numbers in French. It was quite the gayest, most highly charged evening of my tour. The expectancy of imminent war had the capacity to push the audience to the utmost enthusiasm; there was an air of defiance and bravado, whatever the future held. I finally fell into bed, exhausted, at about five o'clock. Next morning I took breakfast very late. The talk was of war, which had been declared by both Britain and France. People were turning their thoughts to how to get home. I still had two more nights to fulfil. I was contemplating having to perform to the staff only when I was handed a telegram by a page-boy.
I stared at it uncomprehendingly. It must be a mistake; I had spoken to Kitty earlier in the week. She had been bubbly, excited about her new job, and she had two houses for me to view when I returned home. The telegram was from my mother.
"Regret Kitty killed in tragic fire. Contact me soonest. Love, mother."
I walked slowly from the room, pausing to be congratulated by an elderly couple who had been in the audience the previous night. By the time I reached my bedroom I was shaking. I sank to my knees and prayed to God, in a shaky voice, that some mistake had been made, or even that it was a cruel hoax. It wasn't.

* * * * * * * * *

Public transport was almost at a standstill, the roads were clogged with military traffic, and there were no phone lines to England. Everywhere was in chaos. It took me over a week to get home, after being marooned for three days in Pau. I missed the funeral. I was desolate and in shock. Sympathy for me was in relatively short supply. Everyone was obsessed with the war, as if within days they expected to be bombed into oblivion or confronted by legions or German storm troopers.

I discovered that Kitty had been treating Evelyn Gibbs for pneumonia. After visiting him she had taken a leisurely walk down to the boathouse. It had been a sunny autumn day, and the trees surrounding the lake were already tinged with gold. The fire was well under way by the time it was spotted and the fire brigade alerted. The police had been called in when two bodies were discovered. It appeared that the gardener's shed had been broken into and a paraffin lamp stolen. A housemaid reported seeing a stranger in the grounds, some time before the fire started. She was certain he was a clerical gentleman.

I reported to the police that Kitty had been harassed by a patient at Shenley who was mentally ill and who posed as a priest. They thanked me. They rang me back the next day. A roll-call had established that no patients were missing.

CHAPTER 17

I returned from France utterly devastated, to find that all places of entertainment had been closed down by the government. With no work to distract me I launched into a three-week binge, in an attempt to blank out my despair. It was during this period that I met Dolores Allingham. Some suggested that I was caught on the rebound, but she had the advantage of being totally unlike Kitty. She had an earthy, motherly appeal, which suited me at the time.

I can't remember proposing to her, but within a year we stood together on the registry office steps, smiling at the world, after slurring our marriage vows. We bought a lovely Georgian house in Highgate. The property market was on the floor, due to the possibility of bomb damage. Luckily, she allowed me to keep this when our divorce settlement was finalised, and it subsequently provided me with much of the capital for my retirement in Spain.

The decline of my career went strangely in tandem with the demise of the Café de Paris. I appeared there finally in 1957, just three weeks before it finally closed its doors. The management could no longer afford to book the top stars. The cabaret alternated between had-beens and wannabes. It was Tommy Steele who became an overnight sensation there. By now my shiny tailed suit seemed as out of date as the numbers I performed. The restaurant was also showing its age; the lights were kept low to avoid exposinging the dirty paintwork, darkened by years of nicotine. The carpets were threadbare and the mirrors tarnished. The guests no longer wore formal dress, most settling for day clothes. The age of elegance had passed. It was a sad week for me, underlining the fact that my career was drawing painfully to a close. There was a conscious move away from the gloom of the post-war years, with its rationing, power cuts and constant shortages. Chance was sought and so many of us were unable to adapt.

Soon I was sidelined from fashionable venues, touring out-of-season coastal theatres and working men's clubs. My earnings plummeted and much of my income was derived from dividends on shares I had brought at the time I was being influenced by Tilly. I discovered I was still quite popular in South Africa, and I went to live there for a couple of years. Returning to England, I found that almost the only bookings I could get were at hotels in Spain that catered mainly for old people. The money was paltry and I hated the life, but at least my food and accommodation were free. Then even this source of income dried up. The old folk preferred bingo! I could, however, see many advantages of living in Spain. The wonderful climate and living costs way below those at home. In 1965 I sold the house in Highgate and moved to the Costa Brava. I congratulated myself when, shortly afterwards, Harold Wilson was elected and stringent currency restrictions were imposed. For several years I lived in some comfort, until inflation began to erode my savings.

I would make an annual trip to London, to look up old friends and meet my accountants. Earnings from my record sales continued to tick over and I even made a couple of radio appearances. Harold Goldman died whilst I was visiting London a couple of years after I had moved to Spain. I went to his funeral at Golders Green crematorium. Although his influence had already declined, there was still a sprinkling of celebrities, most of whom he had helped at some time in their careers. Drinks in his honour went on to the early hours, at a pub in Hampstead.

* * * * * * * *

It was in the spring of 1970 that memories of my childhood and Kitty were brought crashing back into my consciousness. Time had proved to be a great healer and I rarely dwelt on the

past. I had settled into a new way of life, which was undemanding, well regulated and comfortable.
I remember I had been shopping in Oxford Street for some of the things it was impossible to buy in Spain. Cutting through to Bond Street, I was caught in a sudden, violent April shower. Clasping my unwieldy purchases, I ran into the reception area of Phillips, the auctioneers. Not wanting to been seen as overtly sheltering from the rain, I went into an adjoining gallery that was showing a collection of Victorian paintings, due to be sold the following day. Massive oils of haymaking, cows grazing and hunting scenes hung in closely packed rows. Some were darkened, the paint cracked and peeling, whilst others, over-restored, were displayed in unsuitable modern frames. I remember going out to the front door to see if the rain had stopped. In fact, the shower had intensified, although I could see blue sky in the distance. Without much enthusiasm I went to view the watercolours being shown further down the gallery.
"My God!" My voice echoed through the room, and the few other people viewing the sale looked at me with suspicion. Feeling quite shaken, I purchased a catalogue from the porter and then stood in front of the familiar painting. The sad eyes that I had first seen in the kitchen at Theddington over 50 years before looked down on me.
"She's Indian, boy. A princess, I shouldn't wonder," my mother had said. This, though, was no princess, Indian or otherwise. This was a painting of Kitty. The Kitty I knew, beautiful and yet so vulnerable. How had I never made the connection before? With trembling hands I read the description in the catalogue.

Lot 36, Sir George Richmond, 1809-1896.
Portrait of an Indian lady.
Signed and dated 1863.
Gouache heightened with body colour, 24" x 18".

Estimate: £100-£150.

* * * * * * * *

The sale commenced the following day at ten o'clock, and I arrived in good time. I sat with increasing nervousness, as the auctioneer sold the lots with what seemed to me almost indecent haste. The sale had hardly been going for a quarter of an hour before he reached lot 36. There appeared to be little bidding, and I thought the lot was about to be knocked down to me for £80 when a new bidder raised his hand. He bid with the assurance of someone used to doing it every day. His hand rose languidly, whilst I stabbed at the air, my demeanour emphasising my tension and nervousness. A visit to Hatchards art department had informed me that George Richmond had been highly regarded in his lifetime. He had painted royalty together with the rich and famous of his day, including the Brontë sisters. The book on Victorian watercolourists suggested that, currently, his works had fallen out of favour. I had hesitated and another new bidder emerged. I wasn't going to let anyone outbid me. I rose from my chair and bid, walking up and down the aisle like a caged beast. I think it was obvious to everyone that I was not to be outdone and eventually I secured the lot for £340. The languid dealer stared haughtily at me as I went in search of the cashier's office.

Back in my hotel room I propped the picture on my bed, resting it against the wall. It was still in the same old frame that I had pulled from the dark recess of the cupboard at the rectory. Someone had attempted to re-gild it, without any great success. The expression on the face appeared to alter depending on the angle it was viewed from. Worried, frightened, then, under direct light, as if in repose. From whatever aspect, the face before me was Kitty. Perhaps I

should have felt happy with my discovery. Instead my overwhelming emotion was one of apprehension.
I tried to continue my holiday, taking in shows and visiting friends, but I was becoming obsessed by the painting. It was as if the image was trying to convey something to me, and it was worrying me so much that I turned the picture to the wall before going to bed. The following morning, breakfasting in my room, I suddenly felt compelled to remove the picture from its frame. I was convinced that it had something to reveal to me. Washing the knife I had used to spread the marmalade with, I started slitting the dirty paper that lined the back of the frame. Undoing the coarse string used for hanging the painting I stripped the paper away. The backboard was secured by a number of rusty tacks, which I managed to ease with the knife. Placing the backboard aside I gently removed the picture and took it over to the window. There was a faint inscription in pencil on the back.

The Maharini.
Theddington Hall, 1863.
For Revd. G Williamson.

* * * * * * * *

It was pure curiosity that prompted my first visit to Theddington since my mother's funeral. I booked into the Six Packs, which was the only accommodation available in the village. The pub had been renovated but the bedrooms remained dark and cramped. At the time I had lived in Theddington it had only been licensed to sell beers. Now the small dark rooms, where the men of the village had once drank and played dominoes, had been knocked into one large bar. Steak or scampi and chips were washed down with weak keg beer, or hirondelle wine, served by the glass, from giant

screw-top bottles. The village was in transition. Most of the old shops had disappeared, or were run by new owners.
That afternoon I ordered a taxi to take me to the hall. I had rung Evelyn Gibbs and was surprised that he showed little curiosity about the reason for my visit. His clipped voice sounded little changed, although I was soon to discover that his circumstances certainly had.
The main gates to the hall were locked. I had to pay the taxi off and enter by a wooden door next to the deserted gatehouse. It was a long walk up the gravelled drive, which was overgrown with weeds. As I drew closer to the house I could see acres of tiles missing from the roof. The wall to the kitchen garden had partly collapsed and the old bricks lay sadly covered in thick layer of moss. I rang the rusty bell handle and waited. I heard vague movements from deep within the house. I had expected a member of staff to open the door; instead I was caught in the watery stare of Evelyn. As a young man he had towered above me, but, although not stooped, he appeared to have shrunk. He offered no handshake, not even a greeting; instead he beckoned me to follow him. The house smelt damp and I was struck by the lack of furniture, although Evelyn's ancestors continued to stare down from the panelled walls. The library at least was warm, as a log fire raged in the grate, the back plate to which bore the Gibbs coat of arms. We sat facing each other either side of the fire.
"Well?" he said. We hadn't seen each either for over 40 years, and so much had happened, and yet he appeared to show little interest in me or what had prompted my return. In truth, I was non too sure myself. A hunch, a hope, that he could throw some light on Kitty's death.
"Come to gloat, have you?" He thrust forward in his chair, glowering at me.
"I'm sorry? I don't understand."

He launched into an impassioned explanation of how his fortunes had declined, to the point where he was shortly going to have to sell the family home. He seemed to resent my past success and was convinced that I was still extremely wealthy. He was embittered. It was as if, in some obscure way, I had been responsible for his demise.
"You know I went to jail, I suppose?" he said.
I hadn't expected him to mention this. I nodded. The case had dominated the papers for a few days, shortly after the end of the war. He had been accused by some Boy Scouts, who had been camping on his land. The alleged offences were extremely serious, although Evelyn continued to deny the charges, even after his release. It was at this time that I understood my mother's disquiet at seeing so much of him as a boy. In fact, he never made any advances to me.
Evelyn's antagonism towards me seemed only to increase when, changing the conversation, I asked him about the circumstances leading up to Kitty's death. Why, he wanted to know, was I showing an interest now, when at the time I hadn't even attended her funeral.
I explained that I had been stranded in France, but he didn't appear to hear me.
"She was such a special girl," he said.
"I know; I loved her, for God's sake! We were going to be married."
"Rubbish," he snapped. "Remember, I saw her every day for at least two weeks leading up to her death. We were very close. I can promise she had no intention of marrying you."
I couldn't understand his attitude towards me. He was just a sad, jealous old man. I was shocked by how angry I felt "How dare you. We were lovers. I was devastated by her death. I still am."
His watering eyes were in full flow now. "You would have betrayed her soon enough. Your sort always do. Fancy

marrying that frightful woman, so soon after…" His voice trailed away.
"What right have you to take the high moral ground?" I bellowed. "Dib bloody dob, you old poof."
Struggling from his chair, he squared up to me. I felt the heat of the fire on my trousers and the smell of his sour breath. For a moment I was convinced he was going to hit me. Then, suddenly, all his aggression was gone. It was as if the air had been squeezed from his lungs. He fell back into his chair with a jolt.
"I loved her too, you know, since she was a child. I only put up with you because that is what she wanted. She was the nearest thing I had to a daughter."
Moments before I would have ridiculed such thoughts, but now I felt sorry for him.
"Did you know that I wrote to her, twice a week, whilst she was in Edinburgh?" I shook my head
"I was so proud of her when she qualified."
There was a long silence. Not an awkward one, for at that moment I think we both acknowledged the depths of our feelings for Kitty. He shuffled over to his desk and, taking a decanter, poured two generous whiskies.
"One of my last indulgences." He smiled, raising his glass.
"To Kitty!" I said. His eyes were watering again as he repeated the toast. The tension between us had evaporated. We talked about old times, the village and neighbours. Now he was interested in my career, and particularly the wide circle of celebrities I had met. We were on our third Scotch before, tentatively, I raised Kitty's name again.
"Did she really tell you she was not going to marry me?" I enquired.
He hesitated. "Yes, she seemed genuinely concerned and worried."
"About marrying me, or was there something else on her mind?"

"I was just aware that she seemed very tense and not her usual self."
I then told him about the patient from Shenley who had been bothering her. She apparently had never mentioned him to Evelyn, and nor was he aware that a maid working at the hall had reported seeing a stranger dressed as a priest shortly before the outbreak of the fire. I was getting nowhere! Kitty had spent some time with him that afternoon, prescribing a new course of pills to help clear the congestion from his chest. It had been a beautiful day and Kitty had told him she was going to walk down to the lake. She tended to do this after each visit she made, if the weather was good. It was about half an hour after she left that he had first noticed the billowing smoke. Worried, he went up to a servant's room on the top floor, and from there was able to see flames leaping skywards. It had been Evelyn who had rung the fire brigade. Ill though he was, he had run, gasping, to the boathouse. The building was already an inferno. He had to be pulled away by the firemen as he attempted to mount the steps to the entrance, which were already smouldering. He was detained in hospital and treated for severe smoke inhalation.
Surely it was possible, I insisted, that the man found with her was the strange cleric of whom she had been so frightened. Evelyn was becoming agitated again. Certainly, the body had never been identified, and after a lengthy investigation the police ruled out foul play. A verdict of death by misadventure was recorded.
At this point I decided to show Evelyn the Phillips catalogue, with a photograph of the painting I had bought. Going over to his desk, he peered at the picture through a magnifying glass. In the reflection of the light from the open fire he looked frail and vulnerable. His hands were shaking. "It's uncanny, it could be her." He appeared quite breathless. "Oh dear," he kept repeating, short-sightedly studying the picture without the aid of the glass now.

I told him about the inscription and that the picture had been painted at the hall. I asked him if he knew who the maharini was. Several times it appeared as if he were about to speak, but each time he went back to studying the picture.
"What is it?" I prompted. He was no longer the aloof figure who had confronted me on my arrival. He started pacing the room, and I wondered if he had forgotten I was there. He stared out at the overgrown garden.
"My grandfather was a tea merchant; he spent years in India."
I didn't interrupt, anxious for him to continue. The pause seemed to last for ages; he was obviously searching through his memory. "I know he and my grandmother used to give house parties in those days. There were photographs of them in the boathouse."
"I remember; I saw them when I broke in when I was a young boy. Do you recall, the trouble I was in with your mother?"
This fact didn't seem to register with him. "My grandfather was master of the hunt, and then there were the grand picnics and boating on the lake. I know he invited several influential Indian families to the house. He was very conscious of class and breeding, but he had absolutely no colour prejudice. Unusual in those days." There was another lengthy pause. He dabbed at his eyes; they were watering again.
"There was a scandal, you know."
"What sort of scandal?" I enquired.
"It was all very hush-hush, but I did hear my parents talking about it once, but I couldn't make sense of it at the time – I was too young. After my father died I did manage to learn a little more from my mother, although I wish I hadn't."
"Why?"
"Because," and suddenly he seemed angry again, "since Kitty's death I have been haunted by the most ghastly dreams."

"Evelyn, I don't understand; what do your dreams have to do with some scandal that you even have difficulty in remembering?"
I was alarmed to see his shoulders heaving. He was fighting to keep control of his emotions.
"But I do remember. There was a fire then, too."
"A fire?"
"Yes; at the rectory."
"You mean, here in the village?"
"Yes, it must be the same girl in this picture. Who died," he wailed, "in the arms of that bloody priest."
I was alarmed now by the wild look in his eyes.
"How do you know about all this?" I demanded.
"Because I see it almost every night. I am haunted by this recurring image of Kitty or someone who is identical to her being engulfed. He is dark, he looks foreign, he wears strange robes, and round his neck he wears a huge metal crucifix."
Coincidence or not, I was beginning to think that Evelyn was deranged. "Don't upset yourself," I said. I was feeling sorry for him. "I'm sure there must be a logical explanation."
"You don't understand," he said grabbing my arm. "You see, I remember the name of the cleric that my parents had talked about. I know he outraged village opinion, by making himself a nuisance with the wife of a visiting Indian 'nobleman'."
"Well, what of it?"
"The name of the vicar was George Williamson, the same one you say is listed on the back of the painting"

* * * * * * * *

I was intrigued and somewhat alarmed by Evelyn's revelations. Next morning, fortified by a greasy breakfast, I walked down the village main street to St Helen's church. I paused to stare at the rectory. A gravel drive had been laid and a white mini-van was parked outside the front door.

Otherwise, the building stood solid and unchanged. Had the Indian woman been lured to the building, or had she gone there willingly? I found it difficult to imagine the couple over a century before, caught like Kitty in a raging fire. The house must have been rebuilt very quickly, and life in the village had carried on. Within a generation most of our personal triumphs and tragedies are gone and forgotten. Although my early childhood in the rectory had not been particularly happy, I had never been aware of any unexplained incidents, or of forebodings. Was it just because I was an unimaginative child?

I was still much the same as an adult, and lazy, too, with a short attention span. I had come up to Theddington anxious to delve into the past and to try to find out what really happened to Kitty. Now that I had thrown up such a series of remarkable coincidences, perversely my instinct was to walk away. I wasn't even sure that Evelyn was quite sane. Perhaps that was just an excuse; maybe I was more upset and frightened than I was prepared to admit to myself. Before leaving, I decided that I must at least visit my mother's grave to pay my respects. She had died in 1941. I had attended the funeral with Dolores. Cowardly to a fault, I didn't even seek out Kitty's grave on that occasion. All my life I have run headlong from reality. Now, on entering the churchyard, I edged forward through the graves, like a soldier moving through a minefield. With difficulty I overcame an overwhelming desire to turn away. I located my mother's grave, wiping moss and loose leaves from the cold white stone with my handkerchief. Guilt, I have learnt from others, is a common emotion on the death of a parent. I felt it at the time, and it persisted as I placed the flowers that I had bought from the florist into the rusting metal holder. "Sorry, mum," I said out loud. I felt an urgent need to be away from this place, this village. It was all too macabre. Turning, I made a short cut to the road, avoiding the path. My foot caught on a small, unmarked grave, in the form of a cross, which had been largely submerged by earth settlement. I staggered, clasping at a larger, shield-shaped grave. In stopping my fall my hand had been quite badly cut. I pulled out my earth-stained handkerchief, and as I bound the wound I found myself staring at a stark inscription.

Kathleen Curtis.
Died September 2nd 1939.
Aged 28.
Rest in Peace.

I felt sick. Walking at first, then trotting, I crossed over to the path. I felt calmer there. I stared over to her grave. I didn't like to think of her lying in that damp earth, her charred remains, now just dried bones. The two most important women in my life, lying just feet apart, neglected by me all these years. I found my attention being drawn back to the squat, black, unmarked cross. This was surely the resting place of the unknown man found with Kitty. Shivering, with teeth chattering, I scurried into the church. I prayed that morning with a fervour I had never mustered even as a child. I was engulfed by remorse; or perhaps I was only indulging my theatrical leanings, as if, by at last expressing my grief, I would in some way be absolved. Looking up from tear-stained eyes, I was drawn to the list of rectors who had served the parish since 1723. Each was engraved on a separate brass plate. The present incumbent had taken up the living in 1967. Beresford Egan was listed as 1912-1923. I scanned the other plates with a passing interest. One plate had been removed. There was nobody listed for the years 1859-1863.

* * * * * * * *

A lack of resolve, and an inability to pursue matters through to a conclusion, have been with me since I was a child. Self-analysis is supposedly a preserve of the young, yet even now I submit myself to bouts of introspection. I have been, and remain, a moral coward, always seeking the easy option. Having turned up tantalising new evidence about the strange events in Theddington, I ignored them. Just when my interest should have been heightened, I decided to discount the coincidences that Evelyn had raised. In truth I was frightened. I should have pursued my enquiries; instead I returned to Spain and actively tried to relegate the whole business to the back of my mind. I didn't even argue when Maria refused to let me hang the painting in the dining room. It has languished in a wardrobe in my bedroom ever since. Life ambled along congenially for a number of years. I was as happy as I had ever been. I was healthy, well cared for by Maria, and with a wide circle of friends. Days, then months, went by, without my giving Kitty a thought.

Sadly, I had fallen into the trap of many as they grow old, of reading the obituary notices. We dutifully express our regrets, but secretly celebrate as we outlive another contemporary. It was early in 1982 that I read of Evelyn's death at a nursing home, in Harrogate. Another one gone, although he had made a good age. His departure did throw up some unwelcome memories, but only fleetingly as I pursued my well-ordered life.

The first vision was fleeting, too. Disturbing that it came only weeks after Evelyn's death, but I put it down to my subconscious working overtime. Gradually, the images became more frequent and frightening. They were never identical, although Kitty and a handsome yet threatening priest always featured. They developed from jumbled images to detailed, terrifying, pictures of Kitty being defiled, abused and killed. It seemed as if Evelyn's death had triggered the handing of the baton for his horrific dreams to me.

Sometimes, weeks, or even months, would pass without a recurrence, before suddenly images so ghastly would bring Maria running into my room. I sought medical help. I couldn't sleep, pills were prescribed, warm drinks taken before going to bed, and still in no set pattern I was often reduced to tears as the awful images sought me out.

The making of the television programme has given me the opportunity to unburden myself. Catholic friends have explained the therapeutic effect of going to confession, but even this soul-searching has failed. I am still as far away as ever from revealing the truth. Like love, truth is elusive, and I chase only shadows. Perhaps shadows are all I have ever sought.

That's enough of my ramblings. I feel totally exhausted. Now, let's turn this bloody thing *off!*

CHAPTER 18

The *Daily Mail*, October 17th 2002.

Cabaret King Dies

Former cabaret entertainer Mitch has died, aged 91. He collapsed whilst taking part in filming for a documentary on his life for UTV. He was found to be dead on admission to Stratton General Hospital, the town where he had spent much of his youth.
Mitch, a former grocer's assistant, came into prominence in the early thirties as a smooth and debonair performer. His piano playing, which appeared effortless, was meticulous and assured. He had a velvety, well-modulated voice, which instantly evoked a forgotten age. Known for his immaculate dress and exuberant lifestyle, he was linked romantically to film stars and a number of titled ladies. His marriage to the actress Dolores Allingham was short-lived and ended in divorce.
After the war his popularity declined and he lived the last 30 years of his life in Spain. His records continue to sell well and his death is bound to create an increased demand.
The producer of the forthcoming programme, Stephanie Aston, said that she and the rest of the crew were devastated by his sudden death.
Tributes to the singer were coming in from around the world. Sir Paul McCartney and Sir Elton John were amongst the first to express their admiration for his work. Veteran entertainer Hubert Gregg said Mitch would be sadly missed by all that knew him. His was a unique talent that crossed the age barrier.

* * * * * * * *

The *Daily Telegraph*, February 6th 2003.

Last Night On Television

Yesterday's Star

Mitch, the subject for last night's tribute to the former cabaret star, died in the last days of filming for the programme shown on UTV. This added an undoubted poignancy as the frail old man recounted his remarkable story.
His life, from humble beginnings to eventual stardom, was cleverly reflected by the background lyrics of Berlin, Cole and Coward and delivered by Mitch in the clipped tones of the day. Seated at his trademark white grand piano, he was shown playing at a variety of luxurious venues, in London and the south of France. The audiences were interchangeable. Men in white tie and tails, with haughty expressions, accompanied by vapid, glamorous 'gay young things', some blowing languid smoke rings. Behind each table solemn waiters stand upright, like sentries.
Mitch didn't view his past through rose-tinted spectacles. A certain sadness was evident. He gave the impression that he felt much of his life had been wasted, particularly during the period when he was at the height of his fame. Although he was once the highest paid entertainer in the country, he squandered a fortune, living the latter part of his life in reduced circumstances in Spain. He displayed a certain crankiness, alternating with a charm that, when directed at the camera, gave the viewer a glimpse of the extraordinary charisma he possessed and radiated when he was a superstar.
As the final titles went up on screen, Mitch was singing *I say goodbye with no regrets!* I didn't get that impression.
It is understood that Stephanie Aston, the producer of this excellent programme, has subsequently discovered further new material about the singer. This she hopes to incorporate

in a biography, which will be published next year. I look forward to learning more about the life and times of this once household name.

AFTERWARDS

Stephanie thought the old boy had been in such good form. Sometimes it was like pulling teeth just to get him to talk to the camera, but on that last day's shoot he was all charm. He reminisced with enthusiasm. What he couldn't remember he made up. He was incorrigible, but when the mood took him he remained a star. A small crowd had gathered outside the premises where Mitch had worked as a shop assistant when he was a young man. He seemed exhilarated by the prospect of returning to Spain. He was in full flow, rather overcooking it and playing to the gallery. Suddenly, in mid-sentence, he became distracted. His head jerked upwards, eyes widening. For a moment she thought he was play-acting. His hands went to his throat. Staggering, he fell forward, scattering the microphones. A lone woman's voice cried out, followed by a shocked silence as crew-members rushed to help him. He was dead before the ambulance arrived.

She was in denial. She belonged to a generation that doesn't understand death. Growing up without a background of war and infant mortality, the collapse of this old man whom she had come to know so well was sudden, violent and upsetting.

Back in her hotel room, she tried to pluck up the courage to ring Maria with the news. Normally so lucid, she found herself stuttering and making banal, polite conversation. Maria saw through Stephanie's faltering social camouflage.

"What's the matter?" she demanded.

Stephanie had been so cool and professional earlier, but now she wept uncontrollably. "He's dead," she blurted out. Maria made no response. "Maria, I'm so sorry. Are you there?"

There was a sharp intake of breath and a babble of Spanish, and then the line went dead.

* * * * * * * *

The chambermaid let Stephanie into the old man's room. Mitch had neatly packed his clothes into an old leather suitcase. There were a stack of tapes, each numbered, and the album presented to him by the antique dealer on the dressing table. She emptied these into a plastic laundry bag. It was strange being in his bedroom. She could still sense his presence. There was a vague smell of aftershave and something medical – iodine, possibly. The bed was unmade, the sheets tangled, as if he had spent a disturbed night. The pillows still had the imprint of where his head had rested. She placed her hand on the indentation. The cotton was cold. What made her imagine it would have retained some of his body heat?

She was upset that she had not been able to say goodbye to him. From the wary reception he had given her when she first went to visit him in Spain, he had emerged as a warm yet vulnerable old man. She felt he was too harsh on himself, concentrating on his defects. Sometimes his more positive side would assert itself. He could be disarmingly charming. Certainly old-fashioned, and rather pompous too, but he had a warmth that must have been with him always, although he was rather too anxious to deny this.

Stephanie rang Maria again that evening. They were both calmer and subdued. Mitch had left instructions that he was to be buried in Theddington, and Stephanie suggested that she could make the necessary arrangements. She also agreed to pick Maria up from Heathrow the following Tuesday in time for the service.

That evening she started playing the tapes Mitch had recorded. It was very touching, hearing his familiar voice again. She was beginning to realise what a fragile emotional state she was in herself. Things had not gone smoothly in her relationship with Sally, and the death of Mitch had affected her more than she expected. Although fascinated, she was reduced to tears on several occasions listening to him.

Gradually, the significance of Kitty in his life became apparent. She couldn't understand why he had not been more open with her. There was so much more information forthcoming, however, that she felt very encouraged about the prospects for a biography. She contacted a number of leading publishers, to see what interest could be generated. She was contracted to complete just one more programme for UTV, and having been a journalist before entering television she was looking forward to a chance of writing again.

* * * * * * * *

Stephanie hated funerals! She thought there was something barbaric about them, particularly the burial. The church was freezing; the congregation was so sparse that the vicar presumably didn't think it warranted the wall heaters being turned on. Here they were burying a man who had been world-famous a few decades beforehand, and yet the attendance hardly reached double figures, including the vicar and the pall-bearers. Maria, smart in a bright green coat with matching accessories, continually crossed herself, occasionally praying aloud in Latin. The buck-toothed vicar droned on. It was such a low-key end to a flamboyant life. As the coffin was lowered into the damp clay Stephanie tried to make out the names on the neighbouring graves. Had Mitch chosen his plot to be near Kitty? Unfortunately, a northerly wind bore sleet that stung their faces, and they ran to the warmth of a waiting car as soon as the mumbled prayers were complete.

Later, over lunch, Maria alternated between tears and laughter. She hated the service. Why no music? She was a great mimic and did a stunning impression of the vicar. Stephanie liked her. Mitch had been a lucky man, but Maria was not keen on the proposed writing of his biography.

"Let him rest. It's over for him now."

Stephanie told her about the tapes, which surely indicated he would have approved, and Maria agreed that she would leave his papers untouched for her to see when she went to Spain. She wanted to ask her about Kitty, but she sensed that this was not the time.

Weeks later, it was outside Harare that Stephanie first had an unsettling dream about Kitty. She was nearing completion on her final programme for UTV, featuring white farmers who had been turned off their land in Zimbabwe.

Slumbering in an easy chair in her hotel room after a hard day's filming, she sensed herself walking along a seemingly deserted beach beneath a cloudless sky. Turning, she saw Kitty standing by a breakwater, and stalking towards her a black-clad figure. The sky darkened. Looking upwards, she saw it was a huge wave and not clouds that had obliterated the sun. They were all engulfed. Waking with a start, her jeans and blouse were soaked even though the air-conditioning was turned to full volume.

At the time she didn't give the matter much thought, but weeks later, as she finished listening to the tapes Mitch had left, she was struck by the terror that he had felt with his recurring daytime visions. The tapes offered huge new areas for her to explore, but it was his relationship with Kitty that fascinated her. In his mind, her premature death was in some way connected to another tragedy in the village some 80 years earlier. What investigative journalist wouldn't be fascinated by such a prospect? Also, he had left her some really good clues to follow up. She decided to start where she had first met the man, in Spain.

Offers for the book started coming in after the programme on Mitch was shown. She decided to go with Global Press, as they were prepared to pay the largest advance. Indulging herself, she flew business class to Malaga.

Maria was really welcoming. She had learnt that she was the sole beneficiary of the will left by Mitch, so her future was assured. She had left his bedroom and office untouched, and Stephanie was pleased to see the amounts of papers and correspondence that she was being given access to. Firstly, she wanted to find the painting. It was tucked away at the back of a wardrobe, full of racks of suits and jackets, some of which he must have owned since he first came to Spain. For a moment, as she delved between blazers and lightweight suits, she again caught the distinctive smell of the man, masked somewhat by cloying mothballs. Holding the picture, she tried to imagine Mitch as a young boy, staggering out from the hidden cupboard. She took it into the living room, where the light was better. Mitch had spoken in the tapes of how the expression on the face altered depending on what angle it was viewed from. She couldn't see this; to her the look was wary, etched with a hint of fear.

"I hate that picture," Maria said. "It's creepy."

Stephanie asked her if Mitch had ever mentioned Kitty.

"He was a naughty man; he had many women." Her earthy laugh was an endorsement rather than criticism.

Stephanie persevered. "Kitty was special, though, Maria. Were you aware of her?"

She went over to a writing desk and rifled through a stack of papers. "Is this her?" she queried, handing Stephanie a black and white photograph.

The clothes were typical of the thirties and the face smiled out from across the years. "Amazing," Stephanie muttered; it could have been the same beautiful girl. Even the pose was similar to that captured in the painting; only the mood was different. "What can you tell me about her?" she asked.

Maria was scowling. "When we first met, he told me he had only been in love once. All those woman, and just once, you understand." Stephanie nodded. "He never mentioned her as such, but sometimes he had terrible dreams and he would call out her name. It was frightening; he would cry like a baby."

"She was killed, you know."

"Maybe, but she bring him bad memories. You take the picture and the photograph."
"I couldn't," Stephanie protested.
"If not, I will throw them out. Why dwell on bad times? I want to live with happy memories."
Stephanie explained that she needed all the information she could find about Mitch to help her with the book.
Maria looked doubtful. "Well, it's up to you, but I don't understand why you need to crawl over his life. Some things are best left alone."

* * * * * * * *

Stephanie hung the painting on her study wall, with Kitty's photograph tucked into the frame. She felt that they would act as a spur to her in uncovering the truth. The documents she had brought back from Spain had given her detailed information that had not been brought out in the documentary. She had become obsessed to find out if there really was any connection between Kitty's death and the earlier fire. Rationally, she still reasoned that it was merely a coincidence, but she wanted to solve the mystery, so that she could then devote her efforts to the known facts about the man.
Travelling north by car she booked into the Feathers, in Stratton Market. The following morning she went to the library, which had all the editions of the local paper on film, since it was first published in 1837. The paper revealed little about Kitty's death, being more concerned with the outbreak of the war. Details were confined to a brief mention of her death, followed the next week by a report on her funeral, with a full list of those attending. Detailed scouring of subsequent editions made no mention of an inquest. Disappointed, Stephanie turned her attention to earlier editions, to see if she could uncover any details about the rectory fire. On a hunch, she started with film for the year 1859. The *Stratton Gazette*

was a four-page broadsheet, printed in type so small that it was difficult to read on the illuminated screen. Much of the contents was lifted from national newspapers, with a limited reporting of local events. Advertisements were also prominent, with line drawings of fashions and household appliances. The edition for the second week in July revealed what she had been searching for.

Appointment of New Rector

The Revd. George Williamson has been appointed to the living at St Helen's, Theddington, to succeed the Revd. Thomas Collis. Mr Williamson, who is 38, is a classics scholar from King's College, Cambridge, where he obtained a first in Greats. Prior to ordination he spent three years in Greece, studying the workings of the Greek Orthodox Church. For the past four years, the minister has been curate at St. Cuthbert's in Leeds.

At last she was getting somewhere. The following morning she turned up a brief news item from May 1863, informing readers that Mr Augustus Gibbs of Theddington Hall had welcomed as houseguests his highness the Maharaja of Drangadra and his new wife. They intended to use the house as a base for an extended stay in the country. They were accompanied by a staff of some 20 servants.
There was no further mention of the Gibbs or their guests until August 14th. At last!

Fire at Rectory

At two o'clock in the morning last Thursday, flames were seen rising from the roof of the rectory to St Helen's church, Theddington. The alarm was immediately raised and the village engine under the care of Mr Mowbray and Sergeants

Lynn and Taylor hurried to the house. Water was played on the fire for in excess of three hours before the flames were totally subdued, but not before the roof had fallen in. A stiff breeze had made matters worse, with the fire eventually enveloping much of the building. Damage is thought to approach £600. We regret to report two bodies were recovered from the building.

That was it! Nothing more; no further reports, and no mention of who was killed. The honoured Indian guests were not referred to again. There was no report of a new rector being appointed, although there was frequent reference to a Canon Edwards from January of the following year. The trail had gone cold.
Public records were her next line of investigation. After a lengthy wait, a bored-looking clerk eventually turned up the records for 1863. Each entry was made in copperplate, faithfully recording the deaths of local citizens. The pages for mid-August were missing. Not neatly removed but ripped out, jagged edges laughing at her. The department had no record of the vandalism. Stephanie felt uncomfortable, as accusing eyes followed her as she left the building.
Driving back to London that night, Stephanie had plenty of time to contemplate the intriguing situation. Had there been a concerted effort to hush events up, or was she reading too much into it?
Since Harare she had experienced a series of disturbing, unrelated dreams either featuring Kitty or the threatening priest. That night, however, she became really frightened and for the first time questioned the wisdom of carrying on with her investigation. Soon after falling asleep she became aware of a presence. She wanted to open her eyes, but instead she was aware of the breath of a swarthy, bearded figure leaning over her. She was laid out on the altar of Theddington church. Glancing sideways, she could see the congregation knelt in

prayer. Kitty and Mitch were prominent in the front row. The church organ started up, thundering in her ears. The congregation stood. They appeared to be singing, mouths framing the words, but only the organ could be heard. She tried to get up. She felt a sense of panic, but her limbs wouldn't respond. The bearded face was nearer now. She could smell him. A hint of sweat and communion wine. He lifted her nightdress and caressed her breasts. Revulsion, mixed with a sense of anticipation. He smiled at her. Even at that moment, she was struck by his good looks. Thick, wavy hair, full lips and the whitest of teeth. Only his eyes alarmed her. Grey and cold. Slowly he raised his cassock and sent a jet of urine splashing across her stomach. She screeched in silent protest. Thrashing her head from side to side, she saw the congregation were applauding.

She awoke in real terror. The dream had been so vivid she was convinced he was still there in the room. Gingerly she reached for the bedside light. Her nightie clung to her. To her shame, she realised that she had wet the bed.

* * * * * * * *

Her doctor had been sympathetic, to a point. Having been made aware of the turmoil in Stephanie's private life on a previous visit, she had described it as a period of sexual confusion, which Stephanie found patronising. Now the frightening dreams were attributed to an extension of the work she was carrying out for the biography. Her dreams, she was informed, were a form of time travelling caused by haphazard brain activity, possibly of some spiritual dimension, and nothing to worry about. Stephanie became quite weepy. Feeling desperately depressed she left the surgery, clutching a prescription for strong sleeping pills.

Back home she tried to take stock. She had masses of new material. More than enough to produce an interesting book, without getting involved in the coincidence of the two fires. It was crazy to get so upset. Of course, the love between Mitch and Kitty had to be included, but earlier events in Theddington were irrelevant to the story she had to tell. In spite of these thoughts, seated at her computer the familiar painting looking down had an unnerving influence on her. Far from liking the work, she now found it intrusive. The sad eyes followed her round the study. She decided she would sell it and send the proceeds to Maria. For the time being she would hide the picture. Feeling quite liberated, she removed it from the wall and propped it behind the desk. Amidst an untidy bundle of folders and papers littering the floor, she discovered the bulky album the antique dealer had presented to Mitch.

She hadn't even glanced at the book in all the months it had been in her apartment. The outer spine had become detached, but the finely tooled leather covers kept the book intact. Entitled *The British Marine Album*, the book was dedicated to the mariners of England. Each page had a colour print of ships, with apertures for photographs. The ships spanned the transition from sail to early steamers, with their tonnage, length, beam and depth listed. She flipped through the pages, showing only a passing interest in young men in dress uniform pictured outside local houses, whilst children with nannies were captured by fashionable photographers, in Brompton Road and at A & G Taylor, photographers to Queen Victoria. Some of the subjects were very foreign-looking. Dark, swarthy men, massive matriarchs, and a couple of beautiful, raven-haired girls. Closing the book, Stephanie cleared a space for it on her cluttered desk. Swivelling in her chair, she noticed that a photograph had fallen face down on her lap. Turning it over, he was staring up at her. The familiar features were younger and in no way threatening. Tousled, curly hair tumbled over his forehead, covering his ears. His eyes sparkled for the camera. His lopsided smile exposed perfect teeth. It was a modern face; dressed differently, he could have passed for a pop star, or a footballer advertising hair conditioner. His robes were black and round his neck hung a huge metal crucifix. The caption below the photograph read: 'George Williamson'.

* * * * * * * *

The sleeping pills worked! She slept long and sound, untroubled by ghastly images. Within days she was feeling better. She even restored the painting to the walls of her office.

She ran the tapes through again. She found writing positively therapeutic. The early chapters were in place and she felt they read well. Still, the manner in which Mitch died was bugging her. She just couldn't get his final moments out of her mind. On impulse she rang an old colleague at UTV and asked if there was any possibility of seeing an uncut version of the film, at their studio. He wasn't sure, but promised to get back to her. She continued working away, enjoying trying to recapture the atmosphere that the young Mitch would have been exposed to in his early years. She did experience another horrible dream developing during this period, but was able to wake herself up. She was getting on top of the problem. Each day she worked full office hours. There was no socialising. At night she went to bed, tired but fulfilled.

A couple of weeks had gone by when she eventually received a call from Barry, one of the technicians at the studio, who suggested that she come the following afternoon to view the film. It was not just the filming of the death that interested her. She was confident that the uncut version would offer up other information that she had forgotten. Time is the great enemy in presenting television documentaries, and in retrospect it is often thought that what has been left out is of more interest than the material included. The viewing took all afternoon and included two tea breaks before they came to the last day's filming. This was entirely new footage to Stephanie. She knew the clips would upset her, but she needed clarification in her own mind as to whether Mitch had seen something that shocked him just prior to his collapse. Played at normal speed, the film conveyed the confusion caused by him falling headlong into the microphones. A single woman's cry cracked like a shot from a rifle. Stephanie requested that the final sequence be run through at reduced speed.

Barry ran the interview again, without sound. Stephanie leant forward, her lean figure taut with tension. The images were quite grotesque in slow motion. His lips stopped moving, his eyes widening. Were they registering surprise or fear? It was impossible to tell. His hands went to his throat, and then in three-quarter speed he toppled onto the cobbled street. The cameraman had run forward to help. There were crazy shots of cobbles covered in entangled wires and fallen microphones. Then he must have gone down on his haunches to help Mitch. The camera veered upwards over the heads of the crowd, to a window above the shop. Fleetingly there was the outline of a figure, and then a cloudy sky, until the camera was switched off.

"Barry, can you move it back a bit, to where it shows that top window, and freeze it?"

"I'll try," he said. "What are you trying to prove?"

She explained she was convinced that Mitch had seen someone or something that had brought on his collapse. Frustratingly, the image was out of focus and far from clear. She asked him if there was anyway that he could bring the hazy figure back into focus.

"Only by digital image enhancement. You would have to ask my boss."

"But it could be done?"

"Maybe, possibly; I'm not really sure."

* * * * * * * * *

The technical director at UTV was Nick Palmer. Stephanie had met him several times and liked him. Approachable and friendly, he was attractive rather than good-looking. He was charming when she rang him the following morning to ask for his assistance. He informed her he would do his best, provided she agreed to have dinner with him. She groaned inwardly. She presumed he had heard about her break-up with Sally and had joined a succession of men who felt it was their duty to reform this raving dyke. She had not been out socially for weeks, however, and dinner in return for his help seemed a reasonable deal. The date was set for Saturday.

They had a superb meal at an Italian restaurant in Camden Passage. Nick showed a genuine interest in her book project. He had thoroughly enjoyed her programme on Mitch. Their conversation meandered comfortably enough, and yet just underneath the surface she was aware of his interest in her sexual leanings. He was too subtle to mention it outright, but she felt he was trying to encourage her to give him a lead. Stephanie was as confused as ever. She had become disillusioned with men some years ago.

Perhaps she had been unlucky, but most that she had been out with were self-centred and interested only in their careers, acquiring material wealth, and her as a trophy. The relationship with Sally had started purely as a conventional friendship. A sense of emotional vulnerability had brought them together on a physical level. Sex gets in the way of true friendship. They both ended up feeling bitter and guilty.

She hesitated about going back to Nick's flat after the meal. As they drew up outside the Victorian terrace off Holloway Road, she told him she thought she should stay in the cab and go straight home.

“Don’t forget, I have something I need to show you,” Nick insisted, squeezing her hand.
“I’ve heard that one before,” the cabby chortled, turning round in his seat. “Go on, love; he looks a decent bloke to me.”
It was embarrassment that sent her scurrying up the threadbare stair carpet to Nick’s flat. The living room was vintage bachelor pad. Framed posters of old films lined the walls. Two comfortable settees were set either side of an imitation log fire. Indian rugs were dotted around on highly polished wooden floorboards. She was even treated to Frank Sinatra on CD and the lights on the dimmer switch being lowered. Stephanie didn’t feel quite ready for the seduction treatment, however. He poured them each a glass of good red wine. He raised his glass to her. She felt really uncomfortable.
“You have something for me.” Her voice sounded strangled.
He grinned. “For God’s sake, relax. I’m not about to make a grab for you, I promise.”
“Sorry, is it that obvious?” She felt so stupid being that transparent.
“Yes” he added roguishly. She looked quite crestfallen. “Sorry,” he said, grinning. “Here; this is what you really came for, and I’m afraid you are going to be rather disappointed.” He handed her a large buff envelope. She would have preferred to be alone. Somehow she felt he was an interloper in what should have been a strangely private moment. Shaking slightly, she eased the print from the envelope.
“Jesus,” she whispered. The image was fuzzy, but to her in that moment absolutely clear. Staring at her was the face she most feared. He was older, his hair flecked with white. His eyes had a wild haunted look. She felt Nick take her arm.
“Are you OK?” he enquired. She flopped back into the settee.
“Yes, I’m fine. This is rather a shock – that’s all.”

Nick thought the image was still so distorted that it reminded him of a book from his childhood where you had to interpret a series of dots before making up a specific picture.
"At first I thought, what a fierce-looking bugger. Then, looking again from another angle, he disappeared."
Nick was right. Stephanie realised that the image was so fuzzy that, when viewed from different vantage points, she began to wonder if she had seen the face in the first place.
"I'm afraid, once a shot is out of focus, even modern technology can't really bring it back. Anyway, have a look at the other one and see if you can make anything of it. I can't."
"Other one?" Stephanie mumbled. Slowly she drew another print from the envelope. The image was even less distinct. Nick was narrowing his eyes, trying to bring the foggy image into focus. Stephanie could see it immediately. She was petrified. Staring at her was Kitty. Her hand had shot to her mouth in shock. On her index finger was a green scarab ring.
"Nick, do you mind if I stay the night?"
He was an absolute gentleman. He insisted on her using his bedroom, whilst he slept on a settee covered with a couple of blankets. Stephanie lay awake, listening to the endless drone of London traffic. After what seemed like hours she fell into a deep sleep.
She sensed fear and foreboding before the images began to appear in her brain. This time she was unable to snap out of her sleep. The surroundings were familiar. Her own bedroom. It must be a summer's night, for she noticed the windows are open and a faint breeze is billowing the curtains. She is lying naked on her bed and on the opposite wall the George Richmond painting is looking down. The expression of the maharini is one of disdain. Her lips are curled. She is contemptuous and sneering. Stephanie knows he is in the room. She can sense him; whilst alarmed, she is ashamed to feel some excitement. Then he's straddling her, his coarse robes scratching her skin. Pulling up his gown, he thrusts at

her. She cries out in pain, all excitement banished. She hasn't been with a man for over two years. Now she remembers why she hated the experience. He is worse; so brutal, he wants to hurt her.
"Get away from me," she screams. "Leave me alone." At least she can speak! He rams the crucifix in her mouth to silence her, while his pumping becomes more urgent. The metal clatters against her gums and sets her teeth on edge. She manages to work the crucifix free and she screams in terror for her mother.
Nick holds her tenderly. "Alright, you'll be alright now."
She weeps uncontrollably on his bare chest. "Poor girl; you've had a bad dream, that's all."
Ten minutes later she is sitting in Nick's kitchen, drinking hot chocolate. Her teeth are chattering. She still hasn't managed to say a thing. He is very attentive and keeps assuring her that it is just her mind playing tricks. Beneath the pyjamas he has loaned her she feels sore and ravaged. They sit up till daybreak and she tries to describe the background to her fears and those that overwhelmed Mitch. He doesn't try to analyse or explain; he just listens. She is convinced that he will think she is a hysterical woman with a severe personality disorder.
After breakfast he tells her that he wants to see her again. She is amazed after her pathetic performance, and shocked in herself that she is excited by his interest. She feels a need for someone really caring about her. They agree to meet again in a couple of days. They kiss goodbye. At first just a touching of lips, but then the proper job. He's tender. She likes it. She likes him. Maybe, she thinks, there is hope for her yet.
As she is going out of the door he takes the envelope containing the prints and slowly tears them into tiny squares. "Better not to mix with things we don't understand, even if there is nothing in it," he says. She nods in agreement. Now she knows what she must do.

* * * * * * * *

On her way home Stephanie stopped at a garage. She bought a bag of smokeless fuel, kindling and firelighters. She hadn't lit a fire in her flat since she moved in. She didn't hesitate; if she had her resolve might have weakened. Whilst the fire established itself she removed the painting from its frame. She was about to undertake an act of desecration, but her mind was set. The flames were licking up the chimney. It seemed entirely appropriate that the painting should be committed to fire. Holding the picture's edge she lowered the cartridge paper to the flames. For a moment it refused to submit, but gradually the heat blackened the mount before catching and consuming the sketchy lines of the gown. The heat was intense now. With a strange sense of reluctance Stephanie allowed the picture to fall into the fire. First the thick paper blackened, then it curled in on itself. There was a final anguished look before the painting was reduced to black confetti. In spite of the heat from the fire Stephanie felt a distinct coldness in the air. Her short hair was ruffled by a light breeze. A wave of nausea launched itself at her. Bile rose in her throat. She sank to her haunches, eyes clamped shut. No matter; it was done.

Feeling better, she next wrote to Global Publishing telling them that she was aborting the biography and including a cheque for the forward they had paid her. Feeling free and liberated, she asked Mitch to forgive her as she sliced up the tapes he had so painstakingly recorded. Perhaps she should have made them available to the publisher, but she needed to be free to start her life afresh without doubt or fear.

Before completely obliterating her memory of Mitch, she decided to play his final tape just one last time. As she switched the recorder on, the phone rang. It was Nick, ringing to check that she was alright. He wanted to bring their date forward to that evening. He was keen and Stephanie realised she was not only pleased but excited at the prospect. They chatted on for a few minutes, and as she hung up she heard a grumpy Mitch say, "Enough of my ramblings. I feel totally exhausted. Now, let's turn this bloody thing *off!*" She went to take the tape out of the machine. At first she thought it was her imagination, but then she heard it again. He had left the tape running; she could hear him moving on the bed. He let out a deep sigh, and then, clearing his throat, he sang.

It's not the pale moon that excites me
And thrills and delights me,
Oh no, it's you, the nearness of you.

It isn't your sweet conversation
That brings this sensation,
Oh no, it's just the nearness of you

When you are in my arms
And you feel so close to me,
All my wildest dreams come true

I need no soft lights to enchant me,
If you'll only grant me the right
To hold you ever so tight
And to feel in the night
The nearness of you

THE END

The Nearness of You is Mike Hutton's third published book. He is currently working on a novel covering the vice trade in London's West End. He is a part owner of a National Hunt racehorse, and lives on the Leicestershire/Northamptonshire border.